JUNIPER HARVEY AND THE VANISHING KINGDOM

NINA VARELA

LITTLE, BROWN AND COMPANY

New York Boston

Copyright © 2023 by Nina Varela

Cover art copyright © 2023 by Maike Plenzke. Cover design by Jenny Kimura. Cover copyright © 2023 by Hachette Book Group, Inc.

Sword vector © MIKHAIL BALASHOV/Shutterstock.com; sky background © Bur_malin/Shutterstock.com; swirl © ArtMari/Shutterstock.com; cream swirl © Reamolko/Shutterstock.com

Little, Brown and Company
Hachette Book Group
1290 Avenue of the Americas, New York, NY 10104
Visit us at LBYR.com

First Edition: February 2023

Little, Brown and Company is a division of Hachette Book Group, Inc. The Little, Brown name and logo are trademarks of Hachette Book Group, Inc.

The publisher is not responsible for websites (or their content) that are not owned by the publisher.

Library of Congress Cataloging-in-Publication Data
Names: Varela, Nina, author.
Title: Juniper Harvey and the vanishing kingdom / Nina Varela.
Description: First edition. | New York : Little, Brown and Company, 2023. | Audience: Ages 8–12. | Summary: Eleven-year-old Juniper Harvey is having trouble coping in her new Florida town, but when the girl from her recurring fantasy dream appears in her room they have to figure out how to save Galatea's world from a war of rival gods—and deal with their mutual attraction.
Identifiers: LCCN 2022039612 | ISBN 9780316706780 (hardcover) | ISBN 9780316706797 (ebook)
Subjects: LCSH: Dreams—Juvenile fiction. | Magic—Juvenile fiction. | Gods—Juvenile fiction. | Imaginary places—Juvenile fiction. | Lesbians—Juvenile fiction. | CYAC: Fantasy. | Dreams—Fiction. | Magic—Fiction. | Gods—Fiction. | Imaginary places—Fiction. | Lesbians—Fiction. | LCGFT: Fantasy fiction. | Novels.
Classification: LCC PZ7.1.V3963 Ju 2023 | DDC 813.6
[Fic]—dc23/eng/20220906
LC record available at https://lccn.loc.gov/2022039612

ISBNs: 978-0-316-70678-0 (hardcover), 978-0-316-70679-7 (ebook)

Printed in the United States of America

LSC-C

Printing 1, 2022

For the queer kids;
for lesbians young and old,
past, present, and future.
We have always existed
(we will always exist)
in full color.

PROLOGUE

My nightmare is always the same.

Every night for the past month, I've fallen asleep to glow-in-the-dark stars and the lazy spin of the ceiling fan, the sounds of summer rain and peeping frogs, only to wake on a burning mountain under a sky the color of bone.

(I used to have normal nightmares. Ones where I'd do something horrifically embarrassing in front of the whole school, or I was being chased by a snake monster that also looked like my math teacher, or all my teeth fell out. You know, the classics. This new recurring one? Not so much.)

I'm on a mountain that is actively ablaze, the slopes

peppered with small, smoldering fires and charred areas still giving off smoke. The grass under my feet is dead and yellow, rattling in the wind. The sun is a bloodshot white eye. The heat is unbearable. I grew up in Texas, and I've never felt a heat like this, the air scorching my lungs. It feels so real. Somehow, I know this land used to be green and beautiful, but now it's dying.

A woman appears from below me on a winding dirt path. She's young and round faced, with a straw hat shading her eyes. Wildflowers are springing up in the places her bare feet touch the earth, blooming, wilting, and crumbling to ash in a matter of moments. She's leading an odd procession of animals: cows, sheep, and goats mingling with bears and wolves, wild rabbits hopping alongside deer and foxes. There's a stag with a bunch of birds perched on his antlers and a doe carrying an owl on her back. Most of the animals look sick and starved. Their coats are patchy, their ribs showing like roots in soft dirt.

I follow them to the mountaintop, where there's a little stone house with a garden.

The dream changes.

The house transforms into a huge, beautiful temple in the ancient Greek style, with pale smoke drifting out from between its columns like the exhale of a gap-toothed mouth. Then I'm inside the temple. The floor is patterned with black-and-white mosaics. There's an altar at one end, a raised platform with steps leading up to the statue of a god: a towering ivory woman wearing gold robes and a crown fashioned from twisting animal horns. That pale, sweet-smelling smoke wafts from a bronze brazier at the base of the altar. The woman with the magic feet is stoking the flames.

That's when the dream becomes a nightmare.

A cloaked figure enters the temple, their face hidden by a hood. They approach the altar, footsteps echoing on the shining floor. The woman turns, and now her back is to me; I can't see her face. It looks like maybe she says a greeting. As if in response, the figure reaches into their cloak and pulls out a sword—the *biggest* sword I've ever seen, not that I've seen many. And they drive the sword into the woman's heart. The blade punches through her as if she were made of paper, coming out the other side between her shoulder blades. The blood slicking the metal is pure gold.

Thunder rumbles. Storm clouds darken the sky.

Suddenly, there's a warm hand in mine.

The girl beside me is about my age, eleven or twelve. She's got storm-colored eyes, the same roiling gray as the sky. They catch mine and widen in shock, or fear. She opens her mouth, but nothing comes out. White ivory is spreading across her skin. It swallows her like frost, turning her from a living, breathing person into a statue carved from white bone, her face frozen in that fearful expression. Her cold hand is clenched around mine so tight I can't let go. I can't let go.

There's a crash of thunder. The sky bursts like an overripe fruit, unleashing the rain.

That's how it ends.

1

"Miss Harvey. Miss *Harvey*. Miss Harvey!"

Somewhere in the process of twitching violently awake, I knock the pencil case right off my desk. Pens and pencils go flying in all directions. My favorite watermelon-scented eraser bounces away under a cabinet. Half the class starts snickering.

Awesome.

I look up to meet the glowering eyes of the language arts teacher, Ms. Grier. Now, to be fair, Ms. Grier has solid grounds for hating me. In the first week of school, she caught me doodling instead of taking notes. It might not have been so bad if it weren't a doodle of her, complete with a speech balloon that said: *SILENCE, WORMS!*

She didn't take kindly to that.

I've been *trying* not to draw during her class, but it's hard. A lot of the time, I doodle automatically, without thinking about it. And it's just gotten worse since the dreams started. I can't help but draw—in my sketchbooks; on notes, quizzes, and homework; on pretty much any surface that gets within range of my left hand. I've drawn everything I can remember: the mountain, the small fires, the woman and her animals, the temple, the mosaics, the statue, the hooded figure, the giant sword.... And *her*, of course. The girl who turns to ivory. I've drawn her the most.

"Miss Harvey, is there a reason you're falling asleep in my class?" Ms. Grier asks in her wobbly voice. "Are we boring you? Is *A Wrinkle in Time* boring you?"

The true answer: *No. But also yes, because you're teaching it in a boring way.*

"No, ma'am." I'm sure my face is bright pink.

"This is your second offense. One more equals lunchtime detention. Do I make myself clear?"

"Yes, ma'am."

Ms. Grier returns to the head of the room and continues droning on about religious symbolism. I hunch over my notebook, cheeks on fire, and take notes without looking up for the rest of class.

Being the new kid is just constantly embarrassing. It would be less embarrassing if I were a fundamentally different person. But here we are.

The reason I'm the new kid is because this past summer, my family (Mom, Dad, and me) moved from the city of Dallas, Texas (population 1.3 million), to the dinky little town of Cypress, Florida (population 2,300), for Dad's job. I started sixth grade at a new school in a new state, more than a thousand miles away from home. To make matters worse, Riley (my best friend since diapers) has been ghosting me ever since the move. I don't know why. It's like as soon as I wasn't right next door, she forgot I existed.

The thing about starting middle school in a tiny rural town is that you are The Only New Kid. All my classmates have known one another since pre-K. The friend groups? They are set in stone. They are calcified. And, from the bottom of my heart, I would literally rather be sacrificed to a pit of deadly fire ants than try to join a pre-existing friend group without an explicit invitation. I can't even imagine walking up to a random table in the cafeteria and—what? Hovering awkwardly until one of the kids notices me and says, *Uh, hi?* and then everyone's waiting for me to say something, and I open my mouth to ask if I can sit with them, but my voice isn't working. Or worse, I stammer and stutter over the words and nobody can understand what I'm saying, and some pretty girl is like, *Uh, can you repeat that?* and then everyone's laughing, and I have to flee the cafeteria and the school and not stop until I hit the Everglades, where I can live out the rest of my days with the alligators.

No. Nope! Absolutely no way. I'll stick to my sketchbook, thanks.

Later that evening, I'm at the stove making instant mac 'n' cheese when Mom gets home from work. I hear the jangle of keys at the front door followed by the thump of a dropped purse, then the *ka-chunk* of a cowboy boot smacking the wall.

"Juniper Willadean Harvey!" Mom shouts.

Uh-oh.

The shouting is normal—Mom's default volume is a good five notches above everyone else's—but a full name? A Willadean? Yikes. I rack my brain for what I could've done to land in hot water but come up empty. I have no friends to get in trouble with. I'm generally well-behaved. I don't chew on the furniture.

Mom sweeps into the kitchen like a vanilla-scented tornado, tying her hair back as she goes. My mom was born and raised on a farm in rural West Texas and still dresses like it. I'm talking plaid shirts, blue jeans, and cowboy boots, as if she thinks her day might involve wrangling steers. Thing is, Mom is a math teacher at the local high school. Also, we currently live in a swamp.

Speaking of swamps, the only thing I wanted to see here in swampy South Florida was alligators, so you can imagine my disappointment when I found out they don't actually crawl around everywhere like big, scaly squirrels. The town of Cypress is ten miles from the edge of the

Everglades, aka Gator Central, and I guess they rarely feel like making the trip. Which, fair. Anyway, so far the only wildlife I've seen is:

- our next-door neighbor's demonic little Yorkshire terrier (Winifred)
- various sidewalk lizards
- a cute green snake Mom wouldn't let me pick up
- a cute yellow snake I picked up when Mom was out doing errands
- a distressingly large spider (upper-left corner of the back porch) (Claudia)
- approximately ten billion mosquitoes

Florida is basically paradise for mosquitoes due to the high levels of humidity all year round. It's famously infested with them. You know what Texas is famous for? Barbecue.

"Hi," I greet Mom, giving the mac 'n' cheese a stir. "Nice lipstick. Is that Peachy Keen?"

"You've Got a Peach of My Heart," she says. "Don't distract me! How could you not tell me there's a middle school dance tonight? I didn't know until my algebra kids mentioned it. I had no idea! I was clueless! How humiliating!"

"I didn't *not* tell you," I say. "I just didn't...tell you."

"Betrayal! Betrayal from my own flesh and blood!" She pretends to faint dramatically against the counter. Then she pins me with a sharp-eyed look. "Seriously, kid. What's up? Why didn't you tell me about the dance?"

"I forgot it was happening?"

"Uh-huh. Nice try. That's two, so you get one more."

"Um...There's not actually a dance. Maybe you were hallucinating. I think we should take you to the hospital."

"Aaaaand that's three. Truth time."

Ugh. Not to be dramatic, but I already know I'm doomed. I tried so hard to keep the dance a secret from her, but Mom's a strawberry blonde bloodhound—she sniffs out secrets, and once she's got her teeth in something, she doesn't let it go.

"Okay," I mutter. "So, it's a homecoming dance. But that's silly, because homecoming does not matter in middle school. We don't have a football team."

Mom shrugs. "I think it's a small-town thing. The middle school and the high school are right next to each other,

11

and a lot of families have kids in both. My high schoolers do the football game and the fancy dance, and you middle schoolers get your own less fancy shindig—*tonight*, at eight o'clock, which means you have two hours and seventeen minutes to get ready. Phew! That's plenty of time."

I nearly drop the wooden spoon. "Mom, I'm not going."

"What!" Her face goes soft with concern. "Junebug. You'll have so much fun."

But I won't. I know I won't. It's a month into the school year, and I'm still eating lunch alone in the library. I think I was absent the day everyone else learned how to strike up a conversation with other human beings.

"School dances just aren't my thing," I try.

"You've been to *one* dance in your short, little life. *One* does not a sample size make."

I hate math talk.

Mom hip-checks me away from the stove, taking over mac 'n' cheese duty. She rummages in the spice cabinet and pulls out chili powder, Old Bay, cinnamon, and chives. Oh boy. Mom likes to experiment in the kitchen. Mostly her experiments are edible, as long as you don't actually let the food touch your taste buds. I've mastered the art of holding stuff in my cheeks like a squirrel and then maneuvering it so I can swallow without tasting. It's a survival strategy.

My parents are perfect for each other, partly because Dad doesn't even seem to notice when Mom puts half a cup of lemon juice or a tablespoon of nutmeg into a pan of green beans—despite being a pretty darn good cook himself. He hasn't had time to cook dinner lately, though. Dad got hired to work on this research project about wetland soil fertility—that's why we moved—and has to wrangle a team of scientists, so he's been working long hours at home and on-site in the Everglades. Mom has taken over as head chef until his work settles down. I hope we all make it that long.

"Junebug, I think you should go to that dance tonight."

I groan. "But, Mom—"

"No *but*s. Listen, kid. I know the move was tough on you. I wish things were easier. But like it or not, this is our home now. You're gonna be happier once you start planting roots."

"I had roots back in Texas," I say. "Long roots. So many roots. They went deep enough to touch dinosaur fossils."

"There are dinosaur fossils in Florida."

"Mom, I really don't—"

She swats me with a dish towel. "You can't grow roots if you don't water the soil. You can't stay holed up in your own head forever, okay? And you know, I bet you'll surprise yourself tonight. I bet you'll have tons of fun. I really do. When I was a kid, I loooooved school dances. My girlfriends and I would get ready at each other's houses beforehand. I'd do my hair all curly and my makeup all dramatic and feel like a caterpillar turned into a butterfly."

"I don't want to be a butterfly," I protest. "I want to be a cicada. I want to spend most of my life buried deep underground, and once every seventeen years, I'll come up here to eat and scream."

Mom gives me a look. "Stop learning about bugs."

"They're fun to draw! And what's—what's wrong with staying holed up in my own head? It's nice and quiet in there, and I never say anything embarrassing. Mom, please don't make me go."

"You're going." She sprinkles cinnamon into the mac 'n' cheese, and I know that's that. My stomach hurts, and not just at the idea of cinnamon-spiced noodles.

It's not that I don't want the kinds of experiences my mom had. I *do*. And it's not that I'm not lonely here. I *am*.

It's just...I can picture a group of kids getting ready in someone's bathroom, joking around and singing into hairbrushes and all that teen-movie stuff. But I can't see myself in the picture. There's no blank space to be filled; there's nothing missing. I don't fit.

Mom will never understand. She's loud and bright and doesn't have a shy bone in her body. All of my bones are shy. If Mom's a towering, attention-grabbing sunflower, I'm an ordinary dandelion. The eye skips right over me. I'm the backdrop, not the focus.

Now, once upon a time, I had a best friend. I had Riley my whole life, since we were toddlers splashing around buck naked in a pink inflatable kiddie pool. Then I moved to a new time zone. It got less convenient to be friends with me. And just like that, our friendship ended. That's all it took. I think sometimes it doesn't matter how much you water the soil. Still nothing grows. But that's fine. It's whatever, you know? I'm a dandelion. All I need is a sidewalk crack.

Dad wanders into the kitchen then, his square black glasses perched on the top of his head.

"Dinner already?" he says. "I lost track of time." He steals a bite of mac 'n' cheese from the pot. I can see the brown flecks of cinnamon and whatever else Mom added. He chews, swallows, and says, "Mm-mm! That's fantastic. Jo, I don't know how you do it. You've truly outdone yourself."

Mom beams. My parents are bizarre.

2

After dinner, I retreat to my room. Mom offered to help me pick an outfit and style my hair (which is super short, so I don't know how much styling is even possible). But I'm still a little mad at her for making me go to this dance in the first place, so I said no thank you. I'm trying not to regret that. Honestly, I have no idea how to put together a cute outfit. Most of my wardrobe is T-shirts and jean shorts. I have a couple of dresses, but I only wear them if I have to. Dresses make me feel squirmy, like I can't breathe or move right.

It's 6:40 now. The dance starts at eight, but Mom said I should arrive "fashionably late," so we're not leaving the house until eight on the dot. According to my scientific calculations, it will take me five minutes to change clothes and brush my hair. That means I can do whatever I want for the next hour. What I want to do is draw.

The first thing I did when we moved here was figure out which corner of my new room gets the most sunlight. That's where I set up my desk, easel, and art supplies: my paints, pencils, pastels, charcoal sticks, and gummy erasers; sketchbooks and anatomy books; and the set of inking pens I got last Christmas, plus the tablet I use for digital art. I draw basically every day, as soon as I finish my homework. I know I want to be an artist when I grow up, though I'm not sure which kind of artist. I used to dream of being a sculptor, then I decided maybe an oil painter, and right now I'm really into webcomics. In fact, I recently finished my first original webcomic. I came up with the story, designed the characters, wrote the script, and digitally sketched, inked, and colored the whole thing. I'm kind of ridiculously proud of how it turned out.

The story is about a family of mice who live in a pair of sneakers dangling from a telephone wire. One day, a crow pecks at the shoelaces until they break, and the sneakers fall into the back of a garbage truck. The mice are whisked away to the city dump, where they make friends with a family of raccoons and find treasures buried in the trash—mouse treasures like buttons, ribbons, bits of string. The comic is titled *When the Squeakers Lost Their Sneakers*. I haven't shown it to anyone or posted it anywhere. But I could if I wanted to, and that's enough.

Art is my safe haven. Despite what I told Mom earlier, the inside of my head is not always nice and quiet. Sometimes it feels like I'm in a boxing ring, squaring off against the part of my brain that's constantly anxious and embarrassed and sad. When I start drawing, the clanging bells and roaring crowds go silent. My hands are busy making something. My thoughts are focused on the paper, the ink flowing from my pen, the smears of watercolor, the digital brush. My heart settles. The noise stops. I can breathe.

Since I finished my first comic, I've been working on concept art for my next one. It's going to be longer and more complicated, with lots of cool world building and fantasy vibes. It's called *Cicadaland* and is about an underground city of cicadas and other bugs, where the buildings are tree roots and mushrooms and fossils. The first arc follows a cicada named Shriek, who falls in love with a honeybee living in the Aboveworld, the land of fresh air, flowers, and sunlight. Right now I'm doing character design, figuring out what the protagonists are going to look like. I think Poppy, the honeybee, should wear a flower-petal crown.

I sit at my desk, trying to ignore the pre-dance jitters in my stomach. I leaf through my sketchbook until I land on a drawing of the temple statue. The god with the twisting, branching crown. When I first started having the dreams, I assumed the statue was made of marble. After some research—Dad taught me well—I now think it's a chryselephantine statue, which means it's made out of pieces of carved ivory that cover a big wooden frame. That's another thing that makes me wonder about the dreams. I didn't know anything about chryselephantine statues until I did some googling, but the one in the dream has been incredibly detailed since day one. I can see the seams where the pieces of ivory meet, like faint cracks in an eggshell. The only difference from real life is that the statue in the dream isn't painted. (Fun art history fact: A lot of the ancient Greek and Roman statues you see in museums were not always plain white marble. They were often painted in vibrant colors, only the paint didn't stand the test of time.) How did my brain make those specific details?

I turn the page to a drawing of the girl.

The girl.

She's frowning up at me. I've only ever drawn the version of her before she turns to ivory, before her blushing tawny skin turns to hard, white bone. In the dream, I want to ask: *Who are you? Where are we? Why are we holding hands?* But my voice doesn't work. My tongue's as frozen as hers. I don't transform into a statue, yet I'm silent as death.

I turn to a fresh page in my sketchbook and begin to draw. The jitters leach away. I'm shading in the flower petal on Poppy's head when my phone alarm goes off.

Time to get ready.

I spend a minute deliberating in front of my closet, then grab a white blouse and a long jean skirt. My hair is extra fluffy today, like a reddish-brown acorn cap. Or just a bird's nest. I run a brush through it, which has the fun effect of making it even fluffier. I give up.

A knock at the door. "June?" says Dad.

"Come in."

He steps inside, shutting the door quietly behind him. His glasses have migrated from the top of his head to the collar of his shirt. He looks exhausted, bags under his eyes.

It hits me all at once how much I miss him.

Back home in Texas, Dad drove me to school every morning. I always wanted to listen to music during the car ride, while he always wanted to have a conversation. At the time, I found it annoying—it was six AM; the last thing I wanted to do was use my brain. Here in Cypress, I take the bus to school. I can put my earbuds in and listen to all the music I want.

I miss Dad's morning chatter.

He gives me a commiserating smile. "School dance, huh?"

I make a *bleh* face in return. "Mom said I have to go. *Unless...?*"

"Sorry, no allies here. I agree with your mom. I think this is one of those things where it might seem intimidating, or even scary, but once you get there it won't be nearly as bad as you thought. Sometimes it's important to do things like that. Not always, but sometimes."

My last hope snuffs out. "Okay. Yeah."

"June." His tone makes me look over at him. Dad and I have the same brown eyes, but I think his are nicer and warmer than mine. "You are a really good kid. You're kind and thoughtful and funny. You're a good listener. You have fun interests. You pay attention to the world and the people around you. Anyone would be lucky to be your friend. Okay? I mean that."

I stare at a random spot of wall, vision blurry. I can't seem to unstick my throat. Finally, I nod.

"Just be yourself," says Dad. I nod again.

"Ready, Junebug?" Mom calls from the hall.

I clear my throat. "I—I think so!"

Dad gives me two thumbs-up. I respond with a shaky smile. "You'll do great," he says. "When in doubt, just show off all the rockin' dance moves you've learned from your old dad."

"Oh no," I groan, hiding my face in my hands, and he laughs.

3

The homecoming-but-not-really dance is held in the gym. The basketball hoops are strung with paper streamers, there's a disco ball tossing up a rotating night sky, and black lights make everyone's teeth glow a ghostly neon purple. The speakers are blasting a mix of Top 40 hits with the cuss words bleeped out and '80s and '90s throwback songs. Parent chaperones mill in the corners, and there's a table with chips, cookies, and punch. With a few exceptions, the girls have gravitated onto the dance floor (center court) and the boys are huddling like penguins along the walls.

And me? I am hovering near the snack table. Yes,

it does occur to me that my strategy for making friends probably shouldn't be Hungry Crocodile Lurks Below Surface of Watering Hole, Awaits Arrival of Hapless Gazelle, but it's the only strategy I've got. Also, it is worth noting that in terms of evolution, crocodiles have stayed the same for like two hundred million years. Possibly they are onto something.

I take a gulp of punch, washing down a fourth oatmeal-raisin cookie. The song changes to the one where you do the electric slide. A group of bold, adventurous boys break away from the main huddle and hit the dance floor, laughing and shoving at one another.

Last year, at the first school dance we ever went to, my best friend Riley slow danced three times with three different boys. She smiled and ducked her head when each song ended, effortlessly cute in the way of girls who are not me. I didn't understand the urge to slow dance then, and I don't understand it now. Slow dancing in middle school is just holding someone at arm's length and stepping from side to side while avoiding all eye contact. What's the point? I have never in my life wanted some boy's sweaty palms on my waist.

I scan the gym for the millionth time, searching for

any other loners, but everyone's in groups. God. Okay. I'm about to call it quits and go hide in a bathroom when two kids peel away from the dance floor, making a beeline for the snack table. One I recognize as Oliver Xu from my geography class. The other I don't know.

"...tens of *millions* of light-years away," the girl's saying, her voice raised over the music. "Isn't that fascinating? Can you even imagine? Oh, and today Dad hinted that my birthday gift is a Celestron. A Celestron!"

"Whoa," Oliver says around a mouthful of cookie. "What are you even gonna do?"

"Perish," the girl says seriously. "I will perish."

"But if you perish, you can't use the Celestron."

"I'll perish, and then I'll come back to life just to use it."

"Maybe your ghost could use it."

"But if I'm a ghost without a physical body, I can't record my findings."

"Unless," he says, "you find a ghost trainer and practice really hard until you're the kind of ghost that can do telekinesis things. That would be so sick. We could go around haunting people. Hey, you're the new girl, right?"

I realize he's talking to *me*. My head whips around from

where I was staring blankly at the dance floor, pretending like I wasn't eavesdropping. "I...what?"

Smooth, June.

Oliver gives me a crooked smile. Like, naturally crooked, his mouth pulling up higher on one side. "You're in my geography class, right? I'm Oliver. Ollie."

"I'm Juniper. June," I manage.

"Sam," says the girl. "Technically Samantha, if we're doing full names, but that's just wrong."

"Nice, um, nice to meet you." I search frantically for something cool, funny, or interesting. "I—I like your shirt...dress...thing."

Sam glances down at her outfit. "I think it's a romper?" she says. "I don't know. Mostly it just makes it hard to go to the bathroom. I feel like I'm wearing a onesie."

"It's a cute onesie," I say, which is true. It's purple with a moon-and-stars pattern, and she's got matching star-shaped hair bobbles tying back her coily buns. "Um. Do you—do you guys like...dances? Dancing?" Oh my god.

"Oh yeah," says Ollie. "You should see Sam doing the robot. She kills it."

"It's the only dance move I can do." Sam's eyes are

solemn behind her gold-wire glasses. "But I am very good at it."

"You're like freakishly good at it," says Ollie. "I wouldn't be surprised if you were secretly a robot this whole time."

"I'd like to be a robot," she says. "I could go live on Mars."

Ollie gives me a look like, *There you have it.* "You should come dance with us." He says it easy as anything. "It took four tries, but I think I finally annoyed DJ Coach J into playing a song by this metal band I'm obsessed with. Nobody's gonna know the words, and we're all gonna headbang our brains out. It'll be great."

My heart leaps. "S-sure, I—"

Suddenly, a big, shadowy *something* swoops down from the ceiling right behind Sam and Ollie. My hand jerks. Punch splashes all over my blouse. "Oh my god!"

"Whoa!" says Ollie. "You okay?"

"Wh-what was that?" I look around wildly. I don't see the shadow anywhere, and no one else seems to have noticed it. Nobody else looks startled or freaked out. They're all just doing the YMCA.

"What was what?" asks Sam.

"It was like—like a huge owl or something!"

"An owl?" Sam frowns up at the rafters. "In here?"

"Yeah, I..." I trail off. They're both looking at me in concern. I just spilled bright red punch all over my white blouse. "Sorry, I—I have to...bathroom."

"Are you okay?" asks Sam.

"Yes! Totally fine! Sorry, I'll be right back," I say, and at long last make my escape from the gym.

4

I don't go to the bathroom.

My footsteps echo in the dark, silent halls. I keep glancing over my shoulder, half expecting the shadowy thing to come swooping out of the dark, but nothing moves. Maybe I was imagining it. Or maybe it really was just a shadow, and I embarrassed myself in front of Sam and Ollie for no reason.

School at night is so weird. It's like a liminal space— you know, one of those in-between places that seem to exist outside of time. Abandoned buildings, dimly lit waiting rooms, gas stations in the middle of nowhere. In a matter of hours, these hallways will be bright and crowded again, but for now it's like I'm walking through the mirror image of a familiar place. The photo negative.

My feet take me to the art room. Safe haven, remember? Luckily, the door's unlocked, and I'm able to slip inside. I'm used to the art room being filled with sunlight and swirling dust motes, so it's extra weird to see it dark and still and silent. All the stools are flipped upside down on the tables. There's a stack of foldable easels in one corner, a big industrial sink along the back wall, and lots of shelves and cabinets of art supplies. I stand there in the dark, breathing in the smells of paint and turpentine, of ink and charcoal, and the jet-fuel stench of rubber cement.

I love art-room smell.

For some reason, that firefly spark of happiness is what makes me start crying. I don't usually cry that easily, but oh my god. Ollie invited me to dance with him and Sam, and how did I respond? I yelled and threw punch all over myself and started babbling about indoor owls.

I choke out a sob—this raw, ugly noise. At first I'm crying about the dance, but then I start thinking about other things, and it's like a ball of yarn unravels in my chest, and suddenly I'm crying about everything I didn't cry about all summer. I'm crying about Riley ignoring my texts. I'm crying about how much I miss her when she clearly doesn't miss me at all. I'm crying about how much I miss home, my real home.

I miss Dallas. I miss driving out of the city into the desert, with its dusty, pockmarked earth, the scrublands of wildflowers and the lechuguilla plants, whose leaves are so stiff and spiky they're called "shin daggers." I miss lying beside Dad on the rough, pebbly ground, gazing up at the night sky and feeling, for a moment, like gravity wasn't as strong as usual. Like if I tried to sit up, I'd fall off the face of the planet and into the luminous arms of the Milky Way. Most of all, I miss the desert colors: the shifting golden light, the reds and oranges and pale browns and yellows of the landscape, the deep purples and indigo blues. Florida is just green. Swamp green.

I press a hand to my mouth. My breaths are starting to come in hitching shudders, and I want it to stop. I want my head to go quiet. I get up and riffle through the supply cabinets until I find paper and a tin of colored pencils. Then I sit down at one of the tables and try to focus on breathing as slow as ocean waves—*in*, two, three, four; *out*, two, three, four.

I can't really see what I'm doing, but that's okay. My

wrist knows how to move. How to sketch out the rough geometric shapes of a head and torso, the sweep of limbs. First the outline, then the details. I've seen the girl who turns to ivory every night for a month. I know her face. It's wide and fierce. Her nose is big in a way that makes me want to draw it from all angles. Her hair is burnt umber, an earth pigment, darker than ocher and sienna. Her cape and chiton (chiton as in the ancient Greek tunic, not the very cute marine animal) are seafoam green.

My head goes quiet. I stop crying. But I am so lonely it aches. It feels like hunger. It hollows me, like scraping the guts out of a pumpkin.

I've drawn the girl in a battle pose, arms raised like a boxer, dark hair wild around her shoulders. She looks like she could fight the world and win. That's why I can't draw her as a statue. This girl should always be in motion.

"Why are you in my head?" I whisper.

Obviously, the drawing does not respond.

My phone alarm goes off, signaling that it's 9:25. Mom's picking me up at 9:30. I put the art supplies away, fold up the drawing, and tuck it into my pocket, then slip back out of the art room.

Mom's red sedan is idling in the school parking lot. I

nearly burst into tears all over again when I see it. "What on earth happened to your blouse?" Mom asks as I slide into the passenger seat.

Right. I was so busy trying to hide my blotchy face that I forgot about the giant red stain on my shirt.

"I spilled some punch."

"My goodness. I hope that washes out. Anyway, are you sure you don't want to stay longer? Don't leave on my account. There is no shortage of funny animal videos on the internet. I can entertain myself for hours."

"I'm sure," I say. "I just wanna go home."

"Hmm." Mom pulls away from the curb. "Well, we can do that. Or we can make a pit stop at Elmo's Diner. I'm craving a late-night milkshake and some onion rings. You in?"

"Can I get a mint-chocolate-chip shake with M&M's mixed in?"

"Sure."

"And Oreos?"

"Now you're pushing it." Her voice softens. "Junebug. It wasn't that bad, was it? Didn't anything fun happen? Any hot goss? Potential new friends?"

We turn down a road with evenly spaced streetlamps.

I count the seconds between each puddle of light. One Mississippi, two Mississippi...If I lean my head on the cool window and watch the side mirror, it looks like the moon is soaring after us over the dark roofs and telephone wires.

"Um. I hung out with these kids Sam and Ollie," I lie. "We danced together. We did the YMCA and the electric slide and stuff. Um, and Ollie got the PE teacher to play this heavy metal song, and everyone was like headbanging. It was so funny."

"Ha!" says Mom, sounding relieved. "That's great! That sounds so fun! Well, y'all should hang out again. How about you invite Sam and Ollie over for dinner? Or a sleepover?"

"Ollie's a boy."

"Don't be so old-fashioned. Boys and girls can have sleepovers. Do you have a crush on this Ollie kid? Is that it?"

"Ew, Mom, no. I mean—not *ew*. He's really nice. But, um. No."

"Huh." She's quiet for a moment. "How 'bout Sam?"

"What about her?"

"Do you have a crush on Sam?"

"Sam's a girl."

"So? You can have a crush on whoever you want. Well,

as long as they're cute. And nice. They have to be cute and nice. You got that, Junebug?"

It's not that I didn't know it was okay. I know my parents. I knew it would be. They've just never said it so plainly before. I feel like my skin is see-through, like Mom can see right through me, past blood and bone to the soft meat of my heart. Last year, I watched Riley slow dance three times with three different boys, and each time I wished it were me. I didn't want to be Riley. I wanted to be the boys.

"I don't have a crush on Sam," I say carefully. "But, um...thanks. I'll keep that in mind."

"Good. That's my girl. And seriously, you should talk to those kids again. Let them know you want to be friends."

"Oh, um, maybe. Yeah. I'll—I'll talk to them."

"Wonderful! Wonderful, wonderful. Good job. Aren't you glad you went and watered the soil tonight?"

"Yeah. For sure."

Yellow light slides through the car, illuminating us in slices. I reach into my pocket and touch the folded-up drawing, rubbing it like a lucky talisman between finger and thumb. Mom pulls into Elmo's parking lot. The red neon sign glows so bright in the dark, searing the word *OPEN* into my mind.

Once I'm back in the safety of my bedroom, I change into pajamas and sit at my desk, unfolding the drawing I brought home from the art room. The girl glares up at me defiantly. She's almost finished but could use some shading and highlights. I set to work, cleaning up the smudged lines of her arms. I really like her face. I like faces that are fun to draw: faces with asymmetrical angles and strong features, or soft round curves, or intense bone structure. I like my own rabbit teeth. I like the bump on the bridge of this girl's nose. I liked Ollie's crooked smile and Sam's glasses that magnified her big brown eyes.

It's way past my bedtime. I have to get up at six thirty to get ready for school. But a feeling tugs at me like a fishhook. I can't go to bed until I finish this drawing.

Finally, I set down the pencil. I meet the silver flecks of the girl's eyes.

"I wish you were here," I tell her.

Then I turn the page facedown and go to bed.

5

I lie there blinking for a moment. It's pitch-black out, barely five in the morning. My alarm won't go off for more than an hour. It's not raining, which is weird—I could've sworn it was a crash of thunder that woke me up. I guess it was a dream. Though, for the first time in a month, I don't think I dreamed of the temple.

My eyes adjust to the darkness. And my blood runs ice cold. *There's someone in my room.* The shadowy figure doesn't belong to Mom or Dad. Heart kicking into overdrive, I try to hold perfectly still, faking sleep. Are we being robbed? Should I scream for help?

The figure steps into the faint moonlight. All thoughts fly right out of my head.

I know that shape.

"Korei nesa te dan?" The girl says a string of unfamiliar words. Then she sinks to her knees on the floor.

I must be asleep. This is just another weirdly vivid dream. I thought I woke up, but of course I didn't. The dreams have never taken place in my bedroom before, but hey, there's a first time for everything.

"...Hi," I say scratchily. "Hey. Wow. You talked. Sorry, I don't speak your language."

Silence. I realize I can see the girl's face, but she probably can't see mine. The space around my bed is dark and shadowy. She says something else. A tiny light flares, like an ember. It burns pale yellow, illuminating part of her throat and the underside of her jaw. Her hand passes over it, and the light disappears. She says, in clear, lilting English, "What tongue is this?"

"English," I say. "Um...what language were you speaking?"

"Arkhean, of course," she says. "Kypris, goddess of Kypros, is that you? Has she captured you? Has she harmed you? Has she bewitched you to forget your mother tongue?"

"Uh, what?" It never takes this long for her transformation to begin. Flesh to bone, girl to statue. Also, why are we in my room? Where's the temple? The woman with the magic feet? "Um, sorry, has—has *who* harmed me?"

"The god of dreams," she spits, as if the name itself is hateful, a bitter taste. "This is the Isle of Dreams, her own domain. We're far from home, Goddess, but fear not: I will save you from this place."

Huh. I don't know what most of that means, but what I'm getting is that she's super concerned that someone's hurt me. Now, I've been wondering if the dreams are some sort of omen. My mom believes in omens big-time. Once, she had a dream that she got in a car crash, and she got into a fender bender the very next day. Considering my dreams involve a brutal stabbing, I've been a bit worried.

"Am I in danger?" I ask.

"Well...aren't you?"

"I don't know, you tell me!"

"Goddess, I'm afraid we don't have much time. Please, you must return with me to the Isle of Kypros. Your home and your people need you. I—we need you."

My ears burn. "Okay, why do you keep calling me *Goddess*?"

"Because you are one."

"Uh, no, I'm not."

"Yes, you are."

"No, I'm not? I think I'd know?"

"Goddess, what has Dreamtender done to you?" the girl asks, and that's about when I get tired of doing this in the dark. I lean over and turn on the lamp. The room floods with light. The girl's eyes lock on my face and blow wide. Her expression flashes from fright to confusion to *recognition* to pure, vicious fury. She leaps to her feet and draws a sword from a sheath at her waist. A freaking sword. The blade arcs through the air and comes to rest with the tip pointed directly at my face, shining bronze.

"You," she snarls. "I should have known you weren't—who are you? Are you a priestess of Dreamtender? Where is your goddess? I would speak with her!"

When I don't respond within 0.0003 seconds, she lunges forward.

"Whoa!" I grab the nearest weapon—the math textbook on my nightstand—and brandish it like a shield. "Calm down! I have no idea what you're talking about!

This is a dream, okay? I'm gonna wake up any second now."

It feels so real. But then, the dreams always feel real.

The girl goes absolutely still. Even her sword stops quivering in the air. It must be the ivory, freezing her where she stands. I guess the dream's ending.

I let my eyes fall shut. I don't want to watch this—ever, but especially now that I've heard her voice. I wish I could have nightmares about normal things, like showing up to school in my underwear.

Something knocks the textbook out of my hands. My eyes fly open. The girl is still here—and still not ivory. *Mathematics Grade 6* is on the floor with a gash tearing right across the cover.

"Did you *stab* my math textbook? What is your deal?"

"This isn't a dream," she says coldly. "What is this? What does Dreamtender want with me, with my kingdom? I care not that you're a priestess. I will fight you."

"I'm not a priestess! Listen, I don't know who Dreamtender is, I don't know who that other goddess is, I don't know who *you* are. I haven't done anything to you. This is my room."

The girl scowls. "This is the Isle of Dreams."

"It's definitely not. This is Florida?" Then I shake my head. "What am I saying? You're not in Florida. This is a dream. You're a figment of my imagination."

"This is not a dream."

"Sure, whatever you say. I'm June. What's your name?"

"Are you *completely* hollow headed?" she snaps. I jerk back a little, stung. "First of all, if you truly think this is a dream, you've got wool for brains. Look around you! Does this look like the Temple of Dreamtender to you? Second of all, I don't care who you are. You're not the one I'm looking for. Where is this place, anyway? Oh, it doesn't matter. I've clearly taken a wrong turn somewhere. Godsall, how troublesome. Well—goodbye."

She does this gesture in the air above her head, like she's grabbing an invisible hat. When she realizes nothing's there, her eyes go round and horrified.

"Where's the crown?"

"The what?" I ask.

"The Crown of Horn. The crown that was *on my head*. Where is it?"

"Um, what does it look like?"

"What does it—" She shoots me a scathing glare. "A large crown made of horn, what do you think?"

I am picturing a trumpet–French horn hybrid. "Haven't seen it, sorry."

Her fingers flex on the sword hilt. "If you've hidden it somewhere—"

"Oh my god, will you chill out?" I say. "I was literally asleep when you got here. I mean, I'm probably still asleep. Because this is a dream. I think."

"Please. I don't know why you've been invading my mind lately, but obviously there's been a mistake, and obviously this, *here*, is real. Not that it matters. I must find the crown."

And she starts poking around my room looking for this crown of hers, checking under the desk and sticking her nose in the closet and dumping out my entire laundry hamper. I don't bother trying to stop her. I'm beginning to think maybe this *isn't* a dream, but...that's impossible, so, *what*.

Then her words sink in. "Wait, what do you mean, I've been invading your mind?" I ask.

No response. She's tossing out the contents of my sock drawer. I pinch myself on the arm and it hurts.

"Am I seriously awake right now?"

"Are you five years old?" she snaps. "Can you not tell the difference between a dream and reality?"

"Shut up, I'm eleven. And reality isn't usually this *weird*, okay? And can you please be gentle with my art supplies?" She continues to ignore me. "What do you need a crown so bad for, anyway?"

"To leave!" she practically shouts.

"Be quiet, you'll wake up my parents!" Mom and Dad's bedroom is at the other end of the house, and Dad snores like a lawn mower, so I doubt they'll hear the commotion. But you can't be too careful.

"Oh, have you finally accepted that I'm real?" She checks under a stack of old sketchbooks on my desk as if they might somehow be concealing a crown, then upends a mug of dry paintbrushes, sending them clattering to the floor.

"Can you *please* keep the noise down? Don't touch the oil pastels. Those are expensive—wait!" I realize what's going to happen a moment before it does. The girl grabs the drawing I left there last night and turns it over. She stops and stares. "Um. I can explain."

"That's not my nose," she says after a hideous pause. "My nose is larger than that."

"It is not." I know for a fact it's not. I spent like fifteen minutes on her nose alone. She's got a magnificent nose.

"I think I'd know better than you would. You've drawn

it far too small. It's throwing off the proportions of my entire face. I barely recognized myself." She's still staring. Then she clears her throat and puts the drawing down with much more care than she took picking it up. "Who are you?" she asks.

"I actually already said," I feel the need to point out. "I fully introduced myself. Like, one minute ago."

She waves an impatient hand. It happens to be the hand with the sword in it, so she also manages to slice clean through the chain dangling from the ceiling fan. The severed half falls to the floor with a tinkle.

"Awesome. Can't wait to explain that to Mom," I mutter. "Uh. As I said, I'm Juniper. June."

"Juniper June?"

"No, like, my nickname is June. You can call me June."

"Why am I here, Juniper?"

"I just said to call me—you know what, never mind. I keep telling you, I'm as clueless as you are. More clueless, even. I don't—I don't know how you're here."

Her jaw clenches.

"Um. This is the part where you tell me who you are," I continue.

"You really don't know?"

"Am I supposed to?" Maybe she's famous or something. Maybe this is an elaborate prank, and I'm secretly being filmed. Maybe my parents signed a waiver.

The girl draws up to her full height. "I am Crown Princess Galatea, heir to the throne of the Isle of Kypros, daughter of King Machus and the sea nymph Meliana. I am on a quest to save my island."

"Oh."

Her nostrils flare. "That's your response? 'Oh'?"

"I'm processing! No offense, but everything you just said sounds bonkers!"

"Bonkers?"

"I—aaaaagh." I groan into my hands. "Okay. Okay. Just…give me a second." I think I've officially hit my weirdness limit. There's no way I can deal with this at five thirty in the morning on an empty stomach. Instead of posing another question that will get me nowhere, I ask Her Royal Highness, "Are you hungry?"

Even just sitting on the floor in the lamplight, glaring into a bowl of cereal like the Cheerios have mortally offended her, Crown Princess Galatea looks regal. She may as well be perched on a golden throne. I can't get over it. She really is the girl from my dreams, the girl I've been drawing obsessively for weeks. She has the exact same nose and sun-brown skin and long, wild hair. The same chiton and sandals, the permanent scowl, the storm in her eyes. The only new feature is the sword.

But how? How is she real?

How is she here?

"Okay," I say after a few bites of Cheerios. "Something very weird is happening, it involves both of us and our dreams, and we—we need to figure it out. Right? I think we should start by telling each other what's been happening to us. The basic facts."

She sniffs. "Fine. You first, then."

"I—fine. Okay. Um, a month ago, I started having this dream. It's the same dream every night. There's this woman—um, I call her the woman with the magic feet because flowers grow wherever she steps. I follow her up a mountain to a house that turns into a temple. Then I'm inside the temple, and this hooded figure shows up and stabs the woman with a giant sword. And her blood is gold. Then— you're there. You turn into an ivory statue. And I wake up."

The color drains from her face. "Someone attacks Kypris?"

"I don't know. Is that the woman—"

"With the magic feet, yes, that's Kypris, obviously. Oh, gods. The dream must be a prophecy. I knew she was in danger, I knew something was terribly wrong, I didn't—"

"Whoa, whoa, whoa. Slow down. Breathe. Start at the beginning. Who is Kypris?"

She takes a deep breath, holds it, lets it out. "Kypris is the goddess of Kypros. Kypros is my island. My kingdom. My home. What does the attacker look like?"

"I—I don't know, I'm sorry."

"How do you not know?"

"Their face is covered with a hood! They're wearing this...cloak thing!"

"What kind of cloak?"

"I don't know, blue?"

"*Is it blue or is it not blue?*"

"No, it's blue, sorry, I just...I'm usually more focused on, you know, the giant sword?"

"What does the sword look like? There are only a few legendary weapons capable of spilling divine blood. Describe it!"

"Oh my god. No. I'm not letting you interrogate me until you tell me what's going on. You said I've been invading your mind. You said you're on a quest to...save your island? Also, for the record, I'm still wondering *how and why you're in my room*."

Her mouth is a hard line. "Let me assure you, I am not here by choice. I was trying to find the god of dreams."

"Okay, how?"

"With the Crown of Horn."

This is literally the most frustrating conversation I have ever had in my entire life. "How does a crown help you find someone?"

"Because it's the Crown of Horn, which was carved from the Gate of Horn on the Isle of Dreams and thus shares the gate's powers. Obviously."

I put my head in my hands.

"What's wrong with you?" Galatea snaps.

"Nothing. Listen, from here on out, can you just assume I don't know anything about anything—"

"Oh, I've already reached that conclusion."

"Then can you *please* actually *explain* what you're talking about?"

"Why?"

As my dad would say: Jesus tap-dancing Christ. "So I can help you."

Galatea sneers. "Please. You're not even Arkhean." Then she seems to remember that, yeah, I'm very much not Arkhean. "Where...where am I, anyway? I thought the Crown of Horn would open a gateway to the Isle of Dreams. Gods-all, how far have I traveled? Have I ended up in Neeve or something? You look a bit Neevish."

"Sorry to break it to you, again, but this is Florida."

"The kingdom of Florida?"

"The state of Florida. In the United States of America."

"I've never heard of such a place."

"And I've never heard of Kypros."

"Kypros," she says testily, "is the largest of the Drifting Isles."

"What's a Drifting Isle?"

"An island in the sky."

My jaw drops. "In—in the *sky*? Like, literally floating in the sky?"

"In the Cloud Sea above the Arkhean empire, yes."

"The sky where birds live?"

"Yes, Juniper. The sky where birds live."

"Oh. Oh my god." I have a terrible sinking feeling

about this. "Galatea...if what you're saying is true, I—I think you're very, very lost. Like, you're very far away from home. Because, um, in this world there's no such thing as Kypros or the Cloud Sea or the Drifting Isles. We don't have any islands in the sky at all. Actually, hold on." I grab my phone and do a quick Google search. "Yeah, no, we just have the regular ocean ones."

"What are you saying?" She sounds frightened.

"I'm saying...you didn't travel to another kingdom. You traveled to another world. You're from a world that has magic and islands in the sky. And that's not this one."

For the first time, she doesn't seem to have a response.

"That's why we need to figure out what's going on." I'm trying to sound calmer than I feel. "And you need to explain stuff to me. Like, why are you on a quest to save your island? What's happening to it?"

Galatea stares down at her bowl of soggy Cheerios. "It's disappearing."

6

W hat do you mean, 'disappearing'?" I ask.

"I mean the island is under some sort of curse or we're being punished by the gods or *something*. I don't know. Nobody knows."

Galatea sets the cereal bowl aside and twists her hands together in her lap, knuckles jutting bone white. "Piece by piece, the Isle of Kypros is dissolving into smoke. My people first noticed it happening along the coastlines. We thought perhaps the cliffs were crumbling, falling into the salt sea far below. But this is not natural. The island is being...eaten away, destroyed, literally going up in smoke. And nobody has any idea why."

"That's awful." I'm staring at her, trying to wrap my head around it. Families fleeing as the land turns to smoke beneath their feet. "How long has this been going on?"

"About twelve years."

"*What?*"

She nods, grim. "Since before I was born. But it's getting worse. These past few weeks, the island's started disappearing faster than ever. I thought we had years before the smoke reached my people's homes, farms, villages—the city—but now...It could be a matter of weeks. Days, even. What happens when the land, our land, disappears out from under our feet?"

"What about your parents?"

She gives me an odd look. "What?"

"I mean...you're a princess. There's a king and queen, right? What are they doing?"

"Oh." She looks away, clearing her throat. "My father—my father went on a voyage to search for answers. He will return soon, but I know not when. As for my mother, I don't know. She belongs to the sea. I live in the sky. I've never met her."

"Then...who's in charge of the island?"

"Me. Obviously."

My jaw drops. "But you're my age. Right? How old are you?"

"I turned twelve last month."

"You're *twelve* and you're in charge of an island? A kingdom of people?"

She's glaring again. "What of it?"

"I—I mean..." I'm trying to figure out how to say *that's completely bananas* without making her mad. "It's just, um, a lot of responsibility. For a twelve-year-old. You're dealing with this alone?"

"I don't need anyone else," she says stiffly. "My kingdom is my responsibility."

"But...okay. Okay, all right. Sorry. Back to the dream. You've been having it, too? The dream about the temple and the woman—Kypris?"

"Yes," she says. "I dream of the temple. But in my dream, I do not see Kypris being attacked. All I see is you. I cannot move. I cannot look away. Something happens—I turn to stone. Then I wake up. I thought...I thought that was the omen. I thought you were the omen, that you were important somehow, a person I was fated to meet.

Sometimes I wondered if you were Kypris wearing a mortal's face—or the evil Dreamtender or some other god. I thought the dream was about *you*. I didn't know...."

"You didn't know Kypris was there."

She looks sick. "I've never seen her. In the dream, I can't move."

My mind races. "So we've been having the same dream. But for me, the dream is about someone attacking Kypris. And for you, the dream is about...me? And you turning to ivory?"

Galatea frowns. "Ivory?"

"Oh. Yeah, I guess it doesn't really matter, but I think you turn to ivory, not stone. Because when it's over, you look exactly like that big statue in the temple. Which I'm ninety-nine percent sure is made of ivory. I looked it up."

"What—what big statue in the temple?"

Right, she can't see it. "There's a big statue in the middle. I figured it was like the god the temple was built for? It doesn't look like Kypris, though."

"Describe it to me."

"Um. A big, pretty lady in a golden robe. And a cool-looking crown."

"*Dreamtender*," Galatea snarls. "Oh, I knew it! I knew she was behind this!"

"Wait, what? Behind what?"

"Dreamtender is the god of dreams. Long ago, Skyrender, the god of the sky and the king of gods, exiled her to the Isle of Dreams—her home, which lies beyond the mortal realm. Dreamtender has resented him, *hated* him, ever since. Thirteen years ago, she broke her exile and challenged Skyrender to a fight. He won and took her Crown of Horn as a prize. And yes, that's the very same crown I seek now—the only thing that can transport me home. But Skyrender needed somewhere to keep it safe, as it's a powerful magical object, so he gave the crown to my father." She puffs out her chest, proud. "My father is a *hero*, you see. Skyrender favored him and trusted him above all other mortals."

"Okay," I say slowly. "So, Dreamtender hates Skyrender. What does that have to do with your island?"

"I cannot say for certain. But I've come to believe the Isle of Kypros is disappearing because something terrible happened to Kypris. She's the goddess of Kypros, after all—she *is* the island. To harm her is to harm the island; to harm the island is to harm her."

Galatea touches the hilt of her sword where it lies on the floor beside her knee. The sun is beginning to rise, slices of light cutting in through the blinds. One sunbeam is falling directly on her head, turning the dark strands of her hair to gold filaments.

"I don't know how it fits together," she continues. "What I know is this: Thirteen years ago, Dreamtender broke her exile. She battled Skyrender in the clouds above my island. Skyrender won her crown and gave it to my father for safekeeping. And right after, the island began to disappear. Dreamtender was, of course, banished back to the Isle of Dreams, but she's powerful. She's an Old God. Who knows what she's capable of doing to Kypris or my island from afar? And..." Her eyes flick to my face, then away. "A month ago, on my twelfth birthday, I broke into my father's rooms. I opened the secret compartment beneath his bed. No one else knows it exists. No one else knows Father was charged with protecting the Crown of Horn. I am the only one he told.

"He forbade me from ever touching the crown, from ever going near it. But it was my birthday, and I was—well. Never mind. What matters is that I touched the Crown of Horn. And that night, I saw you in my dreams for the first time."

"A month ago," I say faintly. "That's...yeah. That's

when it started for me, too. But how? How on earth am I mixed up in all this? I'm not from your world!"

"That, I do not know."

Silence settles over us like a heavy blanket. I have too many questions. I don't understand why she's here. I don't know how to help her.

We both jump a foot in the air when my alarm goes off. Galatea knocks over her cereal bowl. Milk and Cheerios slosh everywhere, and the spoon goes skittering under my bed. "What was *that*?" she asks.

"That means it's time to wake up for school." A horrible thought strikes. "Galatea, you're gonna have to go with me."

"What? Where?"

"Middle school. I'm genuinely sorry."

She crosses her arms. "I'm not going anywhere until I find the Crown of Horn. Then I am going *home*."

"Well, you can't stay here alone. First of all, my dad works from home, and if he sees you, he will definitely have questions. Second of all, whatever's going on has to do with both of us. Right? We need to stick together."

"But I must find—"

"The crown, I know. I'll help you look for it, okay? I'm sure it's around here somewhere."

I'm not actually sure of this. I'm a little hazy on the rules surrounding magical teleportation devices, especially ones that disappear mysteriously when used. But there's no way I'm gonna let Princess Galatea wander around town asking random people if they've seen anything that looks like a magic crown lately.

"Why do you have to go to school?" Galatea demands.

"I just do. It's the law. I can't skip—I'll get in trouble, and my parents will freak out, and it'll be a whole *thing*, and—and we won't be able to look for the crown. Okay?"

She's scowling so hard it looks painful. "Fine. I suppose we should...stick together, as you said. How long does school take?"

"Um. Until this afternoon. But we'll go find the crown as soon as it's over, okay?" My alarm rings a second time. I scramble to turn it off. "And if it makes you feel any better, there's no school tomorrow or the next day."

"I do not plan to be here tomorrow."

"Right. Well, you're here now. We have thirty minutes to turn you into a normal twenty-first-century sixth grader. So, let's get started."

7

Galatea is not a fan of the school bus.

"I've had smoother rides on a dragon," she mutters as we bump over another pothole and lift clean out of our seats, windows rattling when the wheels touch down. The kids in the back go "Wooooooo!" like we're on a roller coaster. "Oh, gods, save me."

"You're not gonna barf, are you? I mean, you're not gonna be sick?" I ask.

"I don't...think so."

"Please, please let me know if that changes."

"Mm-hmm," she says, lips pressed in a thin line. She's starting to go woozy pale and green around the edges, so

I'm not gonna interrogate her about the dragon comment. But trust me, I'm putting a pin in that. If dragons exist in her world, we are going to discuss it.

Galatea's staring out the scratched-up window at the streets of Cypress: the one-level houses with yards boxed in with chain-link fences, front walks lined with spiky agave and bright flowers, hedges trimmed into neat squares. Cars parked at the curbs, beetle-shell shiny in the morning sun. A gas station, a Taco Bell, Presidente Supermarket with the big blue letters. I try to view it through her eyes. I've seen glimpses of her world—the mountains and valley. I wonder if she lives in a palace. I wonder how strange this is to her, how scary.

She's borrowed a pair of my jean shorts and a T-shirt with a picture of an iguana on it. She keeps plucking nervously at the hem of the shorts, twisting stray threads around her fingers until the tips turn red, then white. I made her leave her sword at home, hidden under my bed. She was not happy about it. Maybe she could use a distraction.

"We need a cover story," I tell her.

It wasn't hard sneaking her out of the house this morning. Mom was in the shower (I heard her singing ABBA), and Dad was already in his office. Still, I have a feeling I won't be able to just show up at school with a random girl and not deal with any administrative questions. Teachers can be so nosy.

"Mm." Galatea's keeping her mouth firmly shut.

"We can't tell people the truth about where you came from, so let's pick somewhere very far from Florida. You're from...uh...Bulgaria. Rural...Bulgaria. You live on a farm. A goat farm? A Bulgarian goat farm. And you've never left the farm in your entire life. Which is why you're like this."

"Like what?" she says through gritted teeth.

"You know." I gesture vaguely at all of her.

"*Hmm.*"

"Look, just stick to the story. You've never left the farm, but now you're visiting me here in Cypress. Because of... reasons. Uh, our families know each other. Somehow."

"You're awful at this."

"Thank you, Princess. That is so helpful." My phone buzzes with a text from Mom. I can feel Galatea's stare on the side of my face as I tap out a reply.

"What is that device?" she asks.

"It's called a phone." How am I supposed to explain

this? I don't *actually* know how phones work. "It's a tool you can use to, uh, to talk to people and send messages, but it's also like a library? You can use it to look up—to search for information, or read stuff, or play games, or listen to music.... Basically, it's a tool that can do a lot of different things. I'll show you more later, okay? I don't know if you should look at a screen right now. It might make you feel sicker."

"Can we search for information on where the Crown of Horn is?"

"Oh. No, sorry, it wouldn't—it wouldn't be able to find the answer. It only knows stuff about this world."

"The crown is in this world."

"Yeah, but we're the only ones who know that. My phone only knows what, um, what the rest of the world knows."

"I...see."

"Maybe later I can use my phone to look up how phones work. We can learn together. It'll be great."

"Nothing about this situation is *great*, Juniper."

"Oh, for Pete's sake. It's not my fault we're in this mess. I'm not the one who decided to put on a magic crown and go world-hopping." That makes me remember one of my many, many questions. "How does the crown work, anyway? I still don't get how you ended up here."

"I told you, it's carved from the Gate of Horn."

"Galatea. I am begging you to remember that I know approximately diddly-squat about your world."

"Approximately *what*?"

"Nothing. I know nothing. What's the Gate of Horn?"

She sighs. "There are two gates on Dreamtender's homeland, the Isle of Dreams. One gate is made of horn, and one is made of ivory. Every night, when Dreamtender sends her flocks of black-winged monsters—her oneiroi—into the mortal realm, they must pass through one of the two gates. The oneiroi who pass through the Gate of Horn deliver good dreams and true prophecies. The ones who pass through the Gate of Ivory deliver nightmares and false prophecies."

Okay. Gate of Horn is good, like the crown. And Gate of Ivory is bad, like when Galatea turns into a block of it in my nightmares.

"How do you know if a prophecy is true or false?" I ask.

"If it comes true, then it's true."

"...Right. So, the Crown of Horn..."

"Was carved from the Gate of Horn and has the same properties. It acts as a gate, a doorway, between the Isle of Dreams and my world, the mortal realm. When I put it on, it should have transported me directly to the Isle of Dreams. To Dreamtender. But something went wrong, and I wound up...here." Galatea clears her throat, turning back to the window. She looks a bit flushed all of a sudden. I hope it's not a sign of imminent barfing. "Can't talk. Feel sick."

"Okay, sorry."

Here's something I can never tell her: A part of me is glad she's here. Not even just because of the dreams. This is the first time since school started that I haven't spent the bus ride with my earbuds in, sitting next to an empty seat. Hoping no one notices me, wishing so bad that someone would. Over the summer, I managed to convince myself that I'd be all cool and confident on my first day at Franklin B. Pruitt, that I'd give off this mysterious New Girl Air that would make people want to talk to me, and I'd magically not be awkward if they did. Shockingly, that is not what happened. On the first day, I froze. I didn't talk to anyone. A couple of teachers had me introduce myself to the class, and all I said was: "I'm June. I'm from Texas." I couldn't think of a fun fact. With everyone's eyes on me, I couldn't think of anything at all.

Considering how scared Galatea is for her island, how desperately she wants to return, it's so selfish to be glad she's here. Still, it's nice not to sit alone.

"So, you don't go to school?" I ask Galatea as we make our way through the crowded halls to my homeroom class, dodging overstuffed backpacks and kids darting like fish. It's loud and bright, the typical morning roar—half-shouted conversations, slamming lockers, shoes squeaking on linoleum, the buzz of the overhead lights. The halls smell like lemon floor cleaner and spaghetti. Galatea looks very overwhelmed, though she's clearly trying to hide it, gliding along with her chin held high.

"I do not attend school, no," she says. "I have private tutors for history, philosophy, literature, politics, diplomacy, music, and languages."

Yeesh. What a snoozefest. "Music sounds fun. Do you, uh, play any instruments?"

"Lyre, kithara, reed pipes, and dragon pipes."

Again with the dragons. "What are dragon pipes?"

"Pipes made of hollowed-out dragon teeth."

"Oh. Does it hurt the dragons? Taking their teeth, I mean."

"Of course not. Dragon teeth fall out on their own all the time. In the mountains, you can hardly walk ten paces without tripping over a dragon tooth."

"Oh. Cool. I have one billion follow-up questions," I start, but the bell cuts me off. Galatea jumps, hand flying to her hip on instinct, fingers closing on air instead of the hilt of her sword. Her elbow nearly clocks a passing seventh grader in the face.

"Don't worry!" I say. "That's just the bell. It means we have five minutes to get to homeroom."

"Must everything be so violent here?"

I think that's a bit rich coming from Xena, Warrior Princess, but I keep my mouth shut. "C'mon, we're gonna be late."

We're the last to arrive at homeroom. Heads swivel in our direction when the door opens, my classmates looking curiously at Galatea. I freeze up at once—all those eyes—but Galatea doesn't even falter. She squares her shoulders and lifts her chin and announces to the classroom,

"Greetings, good people of Florida. My name is Galatea. I hail from the kingdom of Bulgaria. I was raised on a farm with only goats for company, which is why I'm like this."

Now the whole class is staring. This girl Hannah mouths, *Wow*. Jake B. raises his hand. Then four more hands shoot into the air like the kids are expecting Galatea to start calling on them.

Thankfully, Mrs. Zhou steps in. "Settle down, folks. We've got a few announcements to go over this morning. Galatea, should you be on my attendance roster?"

"No, she's just visiting for today," I say quickly.

"All right. Take a seat, girls. Bulgaria, that's interesting."

Once we're seated, Mrs. Zhou continues with the morning announcements like usual. I don't even try to pay attention. Everything Galatea's told me so far is rattling around in my head. The disappearing island in the sky, the goddess in peril, the god of dreams and her gates and her crown. It's like when you dump a new puzzle out of the box and stare at the heaps of pieces, wondering how on earth you'll manage to fit them all together. Except this is worse, because I have no idea what the final picture is supposed to look like. And half of the pieces are gods.

The rest of the morning passes smoothly, though Ms.

Grier does make Galatea sit four desks away from me so I'm not "further distracted" by my "little friend." I figured Galatea would be bored out of her mind during my classes, but every time I glance over at her, she's rapt with attention. In second-period science, I catch her peeking at my notes so often that I end up passing her a sheet of paper and a pencil so she can take her own, which she does, writing in a language that must be Arkhean.

The last period before lunch is my favorite: art. I push open the art-room door and take a deep breath, same as I did last night. Was it really just last night that I ran away from the dance to come cry in here? And draw that incredibly embarrassing portrait of Galatea?

"Juniper."

Galatea's stopped in the doorway.

"You okay?" I ask, with a quick glance around the room. The other kids are bustling around the supply cabinets, setting up their workstations. Nobody's paying us any attention. "Galatea?"

"I feel something." She lets me tug her away from the door. "I feel…magic. Here."

"Like, *here* here? In this room?"

"Yes. No. I don't..." She makes a fist with two fingers extended, like a peace sign but with the fingers together, then brings her hand to her forehead and closes her eyes in concentration. "It's the same feeling I experienced when first I touched the Crown of Horn. I feel...I feel as if I'm waking from a dream, but the dream is lingering behind my eyes, like mist before the sun burns it away...."

"What are you—"

"*Shh.*"

I hold back a sigh, shifting to block Galatea from view. Bouncy K-pop starts playing over the speakers. The art teacher, Ms. Jordan, is cool and lets us take turns picking the music. She's definitely my favorite teacher, and not just because she teaches my favorite class. She's young and wears a lot of funky earrings and paint-stained overalls and sneakers covered in Sharpie doodles. She doesn't even care if we listen to music with cuss words in it—even though one time the principal dropped by and she had to scramble to switch songs. She also lets us talk as much as we want, as long as we keep it to a dull roar. I don't talk, but I like listening to everyone else. The buzz of conversation is like a white noise machine, like ocean or rain sounds or static. I like listening to the rise and fall of my classmates' voices, steady as waves.

Galatea's hand drops away from her face—in the nick of time, too, because we're about to be the only ones not sitting down. "Feel anything else?" I ask, herding her over to my usual workstation. "What was that thing you were doing? You know, the"—I mimic the hand gesture—"that?"

"It is a sign used for channeling magic."

"You were"—I lower my voice—"you were doing magic just now?"

"Well, yes. I should think that was—"

"If you say *obvious*, I will scream. Stay here. I'm gonna grab our supplies."

I hurry to the back of the room. We're doing a unit on printmaking, carving designs into slabs of rubber so later we can press them in ink and use them as stamps. I grab two of everything and head back to the station only to find Ms. Jordan talking to Galatea.

"There she is!" Ms. Jordan smiles at me. I wave at her, for some reason. One of the rubber slabs slips out of my hand and bounces off the worktable and onto the floor. I scoop it up quickly, cheeks flaming. "June, I was just telling Galatea that she's got a great tour guide. Galatea, I'm sure you know this already, but June here is a fantastic artist."

My face is on *fire*. "Oh...I...thanks."

"I did know," says Galatea. I can't help but stare a little. She staunchly does not look in my direction.

"Well, I'm sure June can show you what we're doing this week, but if you have any questions, let me know."

Galatea nods. "You have my thanks."

As soon as Ms. Jordan's out of earshot, I lean over and whisper, "Okay, back to you doing magic. You can do magic?"

"How exactly did you think I was speaking in your tongue?"

"In my...? Oh, you mean English. I don't know; it's not like I know how magic works." I think back to this morning. "You mean when you swallowed that glowy light ball thing?"

"'Glowy light ball thing.' I see your artistic talent doesn't extend to poetry."

"You think I'm talented?"

"And no, I didn't swallow it. You don't swallow divine flame."

"Oh. That was fire?"

"Of a sort. Divine flame is the magic of the gods."

I nearly drop my scalpel. "Are you a *god*?"

"Thundering skies, Juniper, of course I'm not. My mother's a sea nymph, remember? A spirit of the sea. Divine blood flows in my veins. I am not a god, nor am I fully mortal. I can summon a spark of divine flame, but... well... only a spark. Enough to cast out my senses, to feel the Crown of Horn *somewhere*, but not enough to know where. It's rather like walking through a garden with my eyes closed, trying to find a specific flower by scent alone."

"But you felt it somewhere in this room?"

Her frown turns to a grimace. "In this world, I think. When I cast out my senses a few minutes ago, I could feel the presence of magic strong and bright as the moon, shining somewhere just beyond my reach."

Honestly, who talks like that?

"I mean, as much as I love the art room, I don't think it's... magic...." I trail off, remembering last night, when I sat here and drew her, feeling that... pull. And later, in my bedroom, the wish I made. *I wish you were here.*

No. There's no way. There is no way I had anything to do with this. Galatea is the one who comes from a magic

74

world. Galatea is the one who put on the magic crown. Galatea is the one with magic blood or whatever. The only thing special about my blood is that it's type B negative, which is somewhat rare. But it's not even the rarest blood type.

Also, I cannot tell her any of this, because I'd have to confess that I made the world's most pathetic, embarrassing wish. So, I'm gonna go ahead and file this under Things Galatea Doesn't Need to Know. Right alongside my schoolbus thoughts and the number of times I've drawn her.

We work quietly for a few minutes. I add leaf veins and caterpillars and a fat beetle to my stamp. Galatea carves swirling clouds all around the edges of hers, then a blobby shape in the middle, which I think is supposed to be the Isle of Kypros. The scalpel is steady in her hand, her lines smooth and clean and almost practiced.

"Have you done stuff like this before? Like, carving?" I ask.

"Once or twice. Not with this material."

"Oh. Then wood? Stone?"

She doesn't answer.

"Galatea?"

"Mm."

"You know how earlier you were talking about the dream gates? And you said something about Dream-tender's...flocks of something?"

"Her flocks of black-winged oneiroi."

"Yeah. What exactly are those?"

"They're spirits who deliver dreams, or nightmares, as I said. In the form of black birds, they fly from the Isle of Dreams into the mortal realm, into our dreaming minds."

Black birds. I remember the swooping shadow I saw last night, the one that startled me into spilling punch all over my blouse. The shadow no one else seemed to notice. Maybe it wasn't just a trick of the light. But why would a dream spirit from Galatea's world show up at a school dance?

None of this makes any *sense*. At least, not on my end. What is my connection to Galatea? When she touched the Crown of Horn, why did she dream about me? Why did we start sharing those dreams?

Why does Galatea turn to ivory the moment that sword pierces Kypris's heart?

That reminds me—before we left the house this morning, I tucked my sketchbook into my backpack. Risky move, considering how many pages are dedicated to doodles of Galatea, but I did also draw a bunch of other stuff from the dream in there—moments and details I wanted to remember, to study up close. Now I'm glad I did. Galatea can't see the dream from my perspective, but maybe she'll see something in the drawings that I can't. A clue, an answer.

Anything.

8

Instead of going to the cafeteria when the bell rings, I take Galatea to the library. I know from experience it'll be nice and deserted for most of lunch period. I grab us a table in the back near the encyclopedias.

"What are we doing?" Galatea asks, looking around at the shelves with open interest. "Are these books? Do you not use scrolls in this world? I thought you said we had to attend a midday feast."

"I definitely didn't use the word *feast*. Please don't expect a feast. And yeah, we're gonna go eat, but I wanted to show you something first."

My heart thuds as I take out my sketchbook. I've never

shown my sketchbooks to anyone, not even Riley or my parents. I only ever show people my finished artwork—not my rough, messy sketches full of mistakes.

"Um, okay, so, I've kind of been drawing the dream. The parts of the dream that I see, I mean. I mean, duh, it's not like I could draw the parts that I don't see. I just mean—"

"Juniper. Are you going to show me or not?"

"Uh. Yeah. Yes." Steeling myself, I open the sketchbook to a drawing of the hooded figure and the woman with the magic feet, who I now know is Kypris, goddess of Kypros. "This is what I see. This is right before the attack, before you turn to ivory. And I have a few drawings of the temple and the god statue—the one you said was Dreamtender?— and a lot of Kypris."

Galatea stares down at the drawing, a muscle flexing in her jaw. "Are you *certain* you've never seen the attacker's face?"

"I'm sure, yeah. I'd tell you if I had. Promise."

"Well, it must be Dreamtender," she mutters.

"What makes you so sure?"

"Because she's the one *behind* the dreams, Juniper. That's what she does. She is the god of dreams and prophecies, of nightmares, and I think these visions we're having are all three. Why else would she force us to live the same terrible moment over and over again? It is a threat. She's saying, *Look at my power. Look at what I can do. Look at what will come to pass unless you give me what I want.*"

"But what does she want?"

"The Crown of Horn. Revenge against my father and against me, for keeping her precious object from her. Gods-all, I'm such a fool. I should never have touched it. I might as well have flung open the door to my dreaming mind and beckoned her inside."

"But...I thought you said the island is disappearing because something happened to Kypris twelve years ago. Do you think we're seeing something from the past?"

"Yes? No. Well, I don't *know*." Frustrated, she runs a hand through her hair. A piece falls to curl in front of her eyes. "It's just a theory. One of many. That's all I have: theories and guesswork and unanswered prayers. I—Juniper, I didn't—I didn't know about the attack until you told me. I've been trying not to—to lose my head over it all morning, because I don't know what any of this *means*. I can't return home until I find the Crown of Horn, and what if I'm stuck here in the wrong world *forever*, and I can't save my people, and no one ever knows that I wasn't *trying* to abandon my kingdom in its hour of greatest need, and I never, never—"

"Hey. Hey, hey, Galatea." I put a hand on her shoulder, not squeezing, just a grounding touch. "Galatea. Take a deep breath. Can you do that?"

Her breath hitches sharply on the way in, stutters on the way out.

"Nice. Can you do another? Like this." I inhale slowly, *two, three, four*, exhale slowly, *two, three, four*. Galatea copies me, head bobbing a little as she counts. She takes another deep breath, and another. "Yeah, good job. Focus on breathing. You're okay."

"I apologize," she croaks. "I don't know what's wrong with me."

"Oh, dude. Nothing's wrong with you. That was a panic attack. Or like the beginning of one."

"A panic attack?"

"Yup. I get 'em sometimes. It super stinks. It is no fun."

"No fun," she says in a small voice. "No, no fun."

"No fun at all. Mom actually took me to a psychiatrist—um, that's a doctor who deals with...brain...stuff—last year because I was getting them like every day."

"Every day?"

"Yeah. It was after I found out we were gonna leave our home, our old home, and move here. I was, um, pretty anxious about it, I guess."

Galatea's brow furrows. "Why did you leave your home?"

"My dad got a new job. Nothing bad happened; it was just a change. A big change. It freaked me out."

"I see." Inhale, exhale. "I cannot imagine leaving my home forever."

"You won't," I tell her. "That's not what this is. You're going home, okay? I promise."

"You can't promise that."

"I know. I do, though."

She lets out a shaky laugh. "Very well, Juniper of Florida." Then she does the same gesture she did in the art room, a close-fingered peace sign. Instead of lifting it to her forehead, she holds it out to me with an expectant look.

"Cypress," I say, copying the gesture. "This town is called Cypress."

"Juniper of Cypress."

"Galatea of Kypros."

She presses our fingertips together, just once. It is the lightest, briefest contact, but I feel a zing of electricity travel all the way down my arm to my elbow, like knocking my funny bone in reverse. Somehow, I manage not to shiver.

"Promised, then," she says.

"Cool cool cool. Cool. Neat." I turn back to the sketchbook, praying my cheeks aren't as pink as they feel. We stay in the library, poring over my drawings, until Galatea's stomach rumbles loudly enough to cut me off midsentence. "Okay, lunchtime for real," I say, closing the sketchbook. "Sorry in advance about the cafeteria food."

"What do you mean?"

"You'll see."

9

We're almost to the cafeteria when a voice snaps, "Miss Harvey!"

Ms. Grier is stalking down the hallway toward us. "Do not say anything," I say at Galatea. "Remember her class earlier? Remember how much she hates me? She's my nemesis."

"Your nemesis is an old woman?"

"*Shush.* Keep quiet and look innocent."

Ms. Grier stops before us and puts her hands on her hips. "It's seventeen minutes into lunch period," she says. "You're supposed to be in the cafeteria, Miss Harvey. I assume you have a hall pass for you and your guest?"

"We're on our way to the cafeteria right now," I try.

"Hall pass, Miss Harvey." She sticks out a hand.

Ugh. "I don't have one, ma'am."

Her cloudy hair quivers in triumph. "I realize you're new to this school, but here at Franklin B. Pruitt we expect each and every student to follow the rules. That is how we avoid *disruptions*, Miss Harvey. There are no exceptions."

"Actually," a voice says behind us, "there are exceptions for lunchtime academic clubs."

It's Sam, the girl I met at the dance. She's carrying a folded-up project display board with a title written in bubble letters across the top. The only word I can make out is COSMOS. "Hi, Ms. Grier," she says, smiling pleasantly. "June's the newest member of Astronomy Club. Our meeting just ended. Right, June?"

"Right," I say.

"Astronomy Club. How convenient," says Ms. Grier.

"Science is my passion," I tell her.

"I was under the impression that *doodling* was your... passion."

"Um. That, too."

Galatea clears her throat. "What nonsensical restrictions you have here. In Bulgaria, we are free to roam any hallway we wish, no matter the time of day."

"I've heard that about Bulgaria," says Sam.

Ms. Grier's hawk eyes flick among the three of us, suspicious. I brace myself to get detention, but in the end, she just says, "Hmm. Well, now that your little club has ended, I expect *all* of you to proceed directly to the cafeteria. No detours. No shenanigans."

"Yes, ma'am," Sam and I chorus. Together with Galatea, we scurry off down the hallway.

I let out a huge breath when we round the corner out of Ms. Grier's sight. "You're a lifesaver," I tell Sam. "I was gonna get detention for sure."

"What did you do to make her hate you?" she asks. "Show up to class five seconds late?"

"Doodled on my notes. Um, to be fair, it was a doodle of her, and it wasn't very nice. It wasn't *horrible*. But it wasn't nice."

"Ooh, yeah, you're doomed. She'll never forget that. My brother had her like nine years ago, and he skipped her class *one time*, with permission, for a theater rehearsal, and she's held a grudge ever since. We saw her at the grocery store over the summer, and she made this sour-lemon face like just seeing him ruined her whole day. I'm Sam, by the way," she says to Galatea. "Are you new here?"

"I am called Galatea," she replies.

"She's just visiting," I say quickly.

"From Bulgaria, right?"

Luckily, we reach the cafeteria before Galatea can launch into the goat-farm spiel, which is becoming steadily longer and more embellished. She's started taking creative liberties. Earlier, she told Jessica C. that Bulgarians ride around on giant dogs, so like, we're one Google search away from being busted. (When I asked her if that was true—for Kypros, not Bulgaria—Galatea said, "Don't be absurd, Juniper. It's a cover story." So, dragons are no big deal, but giant dogs are absurd. My bad.)

Sam leaves her display board by the cafeteria doors. As she puts it down, the panels flap open to reveal the full title: GAZING INTO THE COSMOS.

"Hey," Sam says, sliding up next to me in the hot-lunch line. Galatea's ahead of me, taking a million years to decide between a slice of square pizza or a glop of tuna melt. "You okay? I went to check on you in the bathroom last night, but you weren't there."

I cringe at the memory. "Y-yeah, no, I'm totally fine. Sorry. I, um, I felt sick, so my mom picked me up. But I'm fine now."

"Oh, good. You guys wanna sit with us?" She mis-
interprets my stunned silence. "It's fine if you don't."

"No! I mean, yes, we do. Yeah. Yes."

"Cool." She picks out a fruit cup, examines it, then puts
it back and selects a different one. "I don't like the cherries. Weird texture."

"Same. Wait, Galatea." I grab her a Jell-O cup. "You
have to try this."

"Does Bulgaria not have Jell-O?" asks Sam.

"Uh, no, they do," I say quickly. "But it's not...the
same Jell-O."

Nice save, June.

Trays full, we follow Sam to a table by the windows.
Ollie is there, along with a couple of others I don't know.

"June from geography!" says Ollie.

"Ollie from...also geography." I sit down across from
a freckly blond kid, trying to ignore the flutter of nerves in
my belly, like lamp-frantic moths. It's fine. All I have to do
is not embarrass myself. That's fine.

"Guys, this is June and Galatea," Sam says. "June and
Galatea, this is Ollie, Noah, and Kamaria."

"Well met," says Galatea.

Kamaria lifts her milk carton in greeting, nose buried

in a thick book. Noah, the freckly kid, says, "Wanna see something disgusting?"

That makes Kamaria look up. "It's lunchtime right now. We are literally eating."

Noah pulls out his phone. "So, this summer I broke my arm, right? And I mean *broke* it. I had to have *surgery*. And last weekend I finally got my cast off."

Kamaria lets out an agonized groan. "I hate you."

"And here is a photo of all the dead skin that was under my cast," Noah says, passing me his phone. I look at the photo. That's a pile of dead skin all right.

"Disgusting," I agree.

Galatea, looking over my shoulder, just shrugs. "I've seen worse."

"You have?" Noah sounds disappointed.

"You *have*?" I say.

"More times than I can count." She takes a casual sip from the milk carton I opened for her. Then her eyes bug out. "Gods-all, Juniper, what is this?"

"Chocolate milk. You don't like it?"

She takes another sip. "It's incredible. This must be what ambrosia tastes like."

"Ambrosia?"

"The food of the gods."

I am very aware that the rest of the table is watching this interaction. I'm hoping they chalk up any confusion to cultural differences.

"My grandma makes ambrosia salad for Thanksgiving," says Noah. "With canned pineapple and mandarin oranges and mini marshmallows. And sour cream. It's okay. I don't know if I'd call it the food of the gods."

"Wait, wait, wait," says Ollie. "Go back to the part where Galatea's seen something worse than Noah's skin flakes. What could possibly be worse? Did you see that? There was enough to build a whole other Noah."

"My alter ego, Flaky Noah."

Kamaria mimes barfing into her book.

Galatea drinks the last of her chocolate milk. I slide my unopened carton in front of her, and she gives me a surprised, pleased look. "Well," she says, "I once aided in saving a man's life after he'd lost half an arm to a mountain dragon. It was his own fault, though; he provoked her. And of course the palace physi—ah, that is to say, the *farm* physicians get all sorts. I live on a goat farm."

"She means lion," I say.

"You live on a lion farm?" says Noah.

"No, like, mountain lion. Not mountain dragon." I kick Galatea's ankle under the table. She jumps a little and shoots me a dirty look.

"I thought mountain lions were only native to the Americas," says Sam.

"Right. It escaped from a zoo." I can't believe Sam just knew that about mountain lions.

"And bit a guy's arm off?" says Ollie.

"It was gruesome," says Galatea. "I helped staunch the bleeding."

Noah goggles at her. "Are you serious?"

"I wouldn't jest about such a thing."

"Was there a ton of blood?"

"Oh yes. Almost as much as there was dragon drool." Galatea jerks when I kick her again. "Lion drool."

"How'd you get to help save him?" asks Ollie.

Galatea takes a moment to answer. "Oh, I just, ah, happened to be in the physician's clinic when the man came in. Right place, right time, I suppose."

"I once asked my aunt who's a doctor if I could watch her do a surgery," Noah says sadly. "She said no way. Bulgaria sounds so cool."

"How long are you visiting America?" asks Ollie.

"I don't know," says Galatea, expression clouding over.

"Not long," I cut in. "You'll be home before you know it."

"Homesick, huh?" Ollie seems to be constructing a fortress out of Tater Tots, stuck together with ketchup. "Wait, were you at the dance last night?"

"She just got in this morning," I reply.

"Oh, too bad. It was a great time. We headbanged so hard my brain is still rattling."

Sam looks worried. "Headbanging actually can cause brain damage."

Ollie shrugs. "How many brain cells did you say I have?"

"The estimate used to be one hundred billion, but modern research places the average at closer to eighty-six billion."

"So, what I'm hearing is I could stand to lose a few."

To be honest, I think Ollie's the kind of boy Riley would have a crush on. He's cute and goofy, with a big laugh. Riley got her first crush in kindergarten, and in second grade, she married Justin Baker on the playground during recess. If Riley were here, she'd give Ollie a school-themed code name and text me stuff like, *history was soooo funny today. i love history omg.* Last night she would have danced with him. And I would've watched from the sidelines, burning.

I wonder which boy she likes this year.

"June? Earth to June." Noah waves a hand in front of my face. "Hellooooo."

"What? Sorry," I say. "Sorry. What?"

"I asked if you and Galatea wanna hang out after school? I live one street over, so we can just walk to my house. Kamaria's bringing her Switch, and we're gonna play the new *Starleague*."

"*Starleague Three: Fall of the Red Giant*," says Kamaria without glancing up from her book.

"You in?" says Noah.

"Um..." It figures that the first time somebody invites me over, I can't go—on account of having to look after a magical princess. "I don't think we can, sorry. Uh, my mom said to come straight home." Total lie. Mom would be over the moon if I asked to hang out with new friends. That's the only reason I'm not worried about bringing Galatea home with me.

"No worries," says Noah. "Sam and Ollie, you in for *Starleague*?"

"Can't today. We're going star hunting in real life," says Sam.

"There's no star hunting in *Starleague*; you *are* a star, and the other stars are your allies in the Galactic Campaign, but go on."

"Right. So, last night I was out in the Pod, and—oh, I have a backyard observatory," Sam explains to me and Galatea. "A mini one, for stargazing. My dad built it for me. It's this special dome that blocks out light pollution. I call it the Sky Pod. Anyway, last night I was out there before bed, and I saw…*something* fall out of the sky. I think it had to be a meteor, but it wasn't like any meteor I've seen. And I've seen a lot of meteors." She pushes up her glasses. "It was weird."

"Weird how?" I ask.

"For one thing, I think I know where it landed. Usually you'd have to track weather radar and seismometer data and eyewitness accounts, and even then you'd have trouble narrowing down the exact crash site. But this one was so close, I was able to track one of the pieces after it broke apart. I saw the smoke cloud rise up with my naked eye. And here's another weird thing: I checked the American Meteor Society fireball report page—"

"*Fireball?*" Noah says.

"That's just a word for a very bright meteor. This one was so bright, it definitely counted as a fireball. Someone should have reported it. But there are no new sightings for Florida or anywhere else in the Southeast. I've been checking the AMS page all day, but still nothing."

"Maybe nobody else saw it," says Noah.

"Impossible. Even if I were the only eyewitness, it would've shown up on all the radar equipment for a hundred miles. And look." She pulls up a photo on her phone. It's all black except for a fuzzy white speck in the center. "I took this with my phone camera. That's how bright it was— like Venus bright. It should've been reported to the AMS or the IMO—the International Meteor Organization—or something. There's no way it just appeared and broke apart and fell to Earth without anyone noticing."

"You noticed," says Ollie.

"Anyone besides me."

"Maybe it was a UFO," Noah says excitedly, "and the

FBI's covering it up because they don't want people to know the *truth*."

"That's . . . a possibility," says Sam. "Either way, I'll find out this afternoon. I know the general area the smoke was coming from, so I'm gonna go investigate."

"And I'm helping," says Ollie with a jaunty salute.

Meanwhile, I am ignoring Galatea's increasingly aggressive ankle kicks. "Hey, um, Sam," I say, taking a casual bite of square pizza. "Whereabouts did you see the smoke?"

"Due east," she says. "Can't have been too far out of town."

"We're gonna start at the Old Barn and go from there," says Ollie.

"Oh, cool." The Old Barn is this abandoned barn off the highway coming into town. I've heard it's a hangout spot for local high schoolers.

Hmm.

I tap out a quick text to my mom.

Me

hi hi

is it ok if I hang out with some new friends after school?

we're gonna go to this kid noahs

house and play video games

Mom replies immediately.

Mama <3

Omg! Yes! Omg how fun!
How are u getting there?

Me

his house isn't far from ours. i'll
stop by and grab my bike

Mama <3

Oh perfect! Ok be safe!!!! Be good and
polite! Have fun!! Feel free to invite noah
over for dinner!!!!
Who else will be there?

Me

sam and ollie from the dance
this girl kamaria

Mama <3

Omg! A whole crew!!!!!! Look at u go!!

Junebug the social butterfly!!!!

Have fun! I have staff meeting after school

so let dad know when to pick you up.

Unless its a slumber party!!:D

Me

thank u ilu

i'll let u know

Mama <3

Love ya!!!!! XOXO

As expected, Mom is so desperate for me to make friends here in Cypress that she's being even chiller than usual. I'm certainly not gonna complain.

I tune back in to the lunch-table conversation just in time to hear Galatea say, "...and then, of course, the Three Sisters."

"Is that a constellation?" asks Sam.

"No, no. In my kingdom, that is what we call the moons."

For Pete's sake. Sam's eyebrows are climbing up her forehead. "Moons...plural?"

"Bulgaria's a kingdom?" says Ollie. "I thought y'all had a president."

"I believe it's a parliamentary republic," says Sam. "With a president and a prime minister."

Then they both look expectantly at Galatea. And kind of at me.

We're saved by the lunch bell. "Time to go!" I tell Galatea, springing to my feet. "Um. Thanks for letting us sit here. And thanks for the invite. I hope *Starleague* is fun."

"It will be," says Noah. "*Starleague* is the best game ever created."

"Wow. Um, I'll have to play it."

"Yeah, dude, you and Galatea both. Come help us save the galaxy from Star Eaters."

I don't know if he means it—if he'll still mean it when cool-girl Galatea is gone and it's just me again—but it's nice of him to say.

"Yeah, hate those evil Star Eaters," I joke, and thank all of Galatea's gods, he laughs.

As soon as we're out of the cafeteria, buoyed along by the stream of kids, Galatea yanks at my sleeve. "Juniper, are you thinking what I'm thinking? That mysterious celestial object—could it be the Crown of Horn?"

"No idea, but it's the best lead we've got," I reply. "I already texted—um, messaged my mom, so we're in the clear for this afternoon. I figure we can take the bus home, grab my bike, and head right back out to the Old Barn."

It takes me a few paces to realize she's no longer beside me. I turn to see her planted in the middle of the hallway, paying no mind to the crowd parting around her, arms crossed tightly over her chest.

"Uh, Galatea? I have to go to my locker before class. My locker is this way."

"The Crown of Horn is *elsewhere*," she says loudly.

I scurry back to her side. "Keep your voice down!"

"Please, no one's listening."

"Yeah, but—still. What's the problem?"

"You said it yourself. We have a lead," she says, fixing me with her blazing stare. "We must search for the crown now, *this instant*, not later. What if something happens to it? What if Sam and Ollie find it first?"

"I mean, they're gonna be looking for a chunk of space rock, not a magic crown. But I can't ditch school, okay? I'll get in trouble. It's only a couple more hours—"

"A couple hours in which anything could happen!"

I fight the urge to pinch the bridge of my nose like Dad does when he's frustrated. "We don't even know for sure that Sam's meteor is the crown. It could just be a super-weird meteor."

"It's the crown. I would bet my life on it."

"Okay, nobody's asking you to bet your life on it. That's not a thing we do in sixth grade."

"When I dreamed of you," she says, low and furious, "I thought you were the answer to my prayers. I thought you were a hero, that we were fated to find each other, that you would save m—save my kingdom. I guess I was mistaken."

I stare at her, suddenly blank. Just blank all the way down.

"Stay here, then. Stay here and I'll go. I can find my way east. Your sun does rise in the east, yes?"

"Um. Yeah."

"Wonderful," she snaps. "I'll be going, then. Pity I don't have my sword."

With that, she storms off down the hallway.

I am trying very hard to be patient and understanding with Her Royal Highness, because of course she's worried about her crown and her island and is dealing with a bonkers intense fish-out-of-water situation, but come on. *I thought you were a hero.* Come on.

I am *this* close to not chasing after her.

However...I can think of like five hundred reasons off the top of my head why Princess Galatea versus the World is a truly terrible idea. She doesn't know about traffic safety. She could get hit by a car. She could get lost in the miles and miles of swampland surrounding Cypress. She could get stopped by a well-meaning grown-up with some pretty valid questions about why a twelve-year-old is wandering around alone during school hours, and somehow I don't think the response *I am not bound by the laws of this realm* would go over well.

Or she could find the Crown of Horn. She could put it on and leave this world. And maybe I'd never see her again, not even in my dreams.

"Galatea, wait!"

I catch up with her around the corner. The halls have emptied out. We're the only ones left under the buzzing lights. She's scowling at me, eyebrows bunched into a familiar angry shape.

"You cannot go alone," I tell her. "Listen to me. You don't know this world. You could get lost or hurt, and then nobody's finding the crown. We have to stick together, remember?"

"The crown is my responsibility, Juniper. Not yours."

"Dude. Princess. I don't care about that. Maybe the crown is your responsibility, but *you* are kinda mine, okay? And I—I don't want you to get hurt on my watch. Or like ever, but especially not on my watch."

Something flickers in her expression, there and gone.

"School's over in three hours. Three tiny, little hours. Please just wait until I can go with you. Please."

"...Fine."

10

There's this goofy saying: "Everything's bigger in Texas." I don't know if that's true, but I do know everything was *better* in Texas.

Pedaling away from my house with Galatea perched in the basket of my bike, sword resting across her lap, I'm convinced the heat here in Florida is ten times worse. Sure, Texas is hot as the hinges of Hades, as Mom puts it, but it's a dry heat, like the heat in my dream, where going outside feels like receiving a friendly slap from the sun. Cypress heat feels like wading into a kiddie pool at the end of the day, when the water's so soupy you start wondering about the ratio of chlorine to toddler pee and there are dead bugs and used Band-Aids drifting along the bottom. The breeze feels like dog breath. It's like biking in the sweaty armpit of God.

"I apologize," Galatea says out of nowhere, barely loud enough to be heard over the sounds of my harsh breathing and the crickets rasping in the grass.

"What was that?"

She huffs. "I said I apologize. For what I said earlier, at your school." She tilts her head back, annoyingly sending strands of her hair into my mouth. It smells like sweat and seawater, something flowery. She frowns squintily at the sky. "My actions toward you have been dishonorable. In my life, I have grown accustomed to…well, to facing things alone, and I suppose…"

"You talk fancy when you're nervous," I blurt out.

"Pardon?"

"Like, fancier than usual. Sorry. You don't have to apologize; it's fine."

"It's not fine," she says, directing her frown at me. "On my honor, as crown princess of the Isle of Kypros, I will not treat you so callously again."

"Oh my god. No worries, it's fine."

"Thundering skies, Juniper, do you not understand what I'm saying? Am I not speaking your strange tongue? Who said anything about worries? I was cruel to you. I spoke cruelly, out of anger. *Therefore*, I am apologizing. I would write it out for you in Arkhean, Middle Arkhean, Old Arkhean, four Kyprosian dialects, six languages from the kingdoms beyond the empire—"

"Galatea?"

"Juniper."

"I accept your apology."

"Thank you. Gods-all, but you make things difficult." She's drumming her fingers on the leather sword sheath. "The point I am trying to make is that I keep forgetting I'm not...Look, I'm simply not in the habit of..."

"Accepting help?"

"Yes. That."

"Right. Well, get used to it. We're in this together."

"Yes," she says, a little breathless for someone who isn't pedaling a bike.

"So, um, is there anything else you can tell me about the crown, or your side of the dreams?"

"Hmm. Well, there's the Oracle."

"The Oracle? Remember how I need you to overexplain everything?"

"Right, yes. An oracle is a human who acts as a mouthpiece for the gods, delivering divine messages and prophecies. Ours is the Oracle of Kypros. I'd requested an audience with her a few times before, but this was the first time she had agreed to see me."

"Seriously? You're the princess."

"And she's the Oracle. She acts in accordance with the Fates, the stars, the heavens—not human whims. To become an oracle, you must cut out your heart and cast it into divine fire and let it burn. If a tongue of flame ignites in your chest, preserving your life, you have been chosen by the gods. If it doesn't, well, you haven't."

I gulp and continue pedaling.

"Anyway, she finally agreed to see me. I told her about my fears, my dreams. I told her, 'In my dreams, I turn into a statue. And I see a girl who looks like this.'" Her face twists into a look of exaggerated shock, with bulging eyes and a dangling jaw.

My own jaw drops. "That is not what I look like!"

"That is exactly what you look like."

"Is not!"

"Is too. I practiced it in the mirror."

"Oh my god, actually?"

"I found it rather amusing."

"Gee, thanks." While I've been hopelessly fixated on how pretty she is, she has been imitating my goofy facial expressions to make herself laugh. Great. That is so great. I want to dunk my head in a lake.

Galatea coughs. "The Oracle didn't answer me for a long time. We just sat there in silence. I didn't know what to do other than wait. It's strange, she looks so young—she was only twenty when she became the Oracle—but the space around her feels so ancient. It hangs in the air like dust, the weight of her years. A thousand years. Can you imagine?"

"She's a thousand years old?"

"Nine hundred and ninety-four. Young for an oracle, really, but I haven't met any others, so I was impressed. Anyway. I waited all night for her to speak. Finally, at dawn break, I said, 'Oracle, please. Please tell me how to save my kingdom.' She opened her eyes then. I've never seen such eyes, yellow and hot with fire. They shot sparks. And she delivered a prophecy. She recites gravely:

"Heart and kingdom, land and throne
A goddess sleeps entombed in bone.
To rightful owner must return
The stolen crown, or all will burn."

I look at her. "'The stolen crown'..."

"Indeed. That's what makes me so certain Dream-tender is behind all this. For what reason I don't know, but I know she's involved."

A bead of sweat trickles down the side of my face. Before long, the EZ Stop gas station swims into view. I pedal past it and turn onto the highway, which is just another empty two-lane road. A horsefly bobs around our heads. Galatea swats at it.

"I wouldn't do that if I were you," I pant out. "They bite."

"Eugh. How much longer until we reach—"

The sun goes out.

At least that's what it feels like. One moment, it's a hot, bright Florida afternoon, and the next, we're plunged into total darkness. My foot slips, and the pedal shreds the back of my ankle. "Oh!"

"Juniper. Don't move."

The bike wobbles to a stop. I plant my feet on the asphalt. A crow caws from somewhere high above. Then it's like the switch flips back on. I squint against the sudden brightness to see everything's gone back to normal. We're stopped on the side of the road. It's an early-fall afternoon. The sun shines hotly and the crickets sing.

"What on earth was that?" I ask.

"I don't know." Galatea climbs out of the basket, one hand on the hilt of her sword. "Leave the bike. Let's walk from here."

"We're gonna keep going?"

"Of course. Why would we stop?"

"No reason," I sigh. "Just checking."

I hide my bike in a patch of long grass. We start off down the highway on foot, braced for another bout of that sudden dark. It doesn't come, and before long the Old Barn comes into view, half hidden behind a thick tree with Spanish moss dripping from its branches. The barn looks like a ghost ship, this big, falling-apart wooden structure in a rippling green sea. The walls are covered in graffiti, the tin roof red with rust.

Galatea grabs my wrist. "I feel something. Magic. Stronger than it was in the art room."

"Okay, that's good, right? The crown is nearby?"

"It must be."

"Nice," I say. "Wow, that was easier than I—"

"AAAAAAAAAAAAAAAAHHHHHH!"

The scream comes from the direction of the Old Barn.

We look at each other and take off running. Galatea unsheathes her sword without breaking her stride, bronze flashing in the sun. I nearly trip over three different empty cans of spray paint lying in the grass. We round the corner of the barn, and Galatea skids to a stop so abruptly I almost crash right into her. That's when things get weird. Well, weirder.

Ollie Xu is being attacked by a flock of flying monster sheep.

11

You might be wondering how I can tell they're monster sheep, despite having never encountered monster sheep before. Easy. The huge, feathery black wings sprouting from their woolly backs are a pretty good indicator, along with the glowing white eyes and the long, curving talons where hooves should be. One of the sheep has its jaws clamped around the end of the baseball bat Ollie is using to defend himself—he's backed up against the side of the barn, surfboard-sized wings beating the air all around him—and is gnawing it like a chew toy, raining flecks of spittle and wood splinters.

"Stay back, Juniper."

Galatea charges. Her sword arcs brightly in the sun, and the sheep scatter out of the way. She spins like a dancer, blade slashing. Two of the sheep explode into a shower of black feathers that wisp away like smoke. The others let out horrible noises that sound like bleats mixed with the screech of nails on a chalkboard and swarm Galatea. She's drawing them away from Ollie. Then I see Sam pounding across the grass toward us. She swings the backpack off her shoulders and starts windmilling it by the straps, like a nunchuck, until something makes her slip and fall hard.

"Sam!" says Ollie. He starts toward her.

"No!" she says. "Don't come any closer!"

The grass around her is wobbling like Jell-O. It turns into a pool of shiny mud before our eyes, Sam's foot stuck in it past the ankle. She struggles to pull it free, but her other foot's also sinking, along with the hand that broke her fall.

"Is that *quicksand*?" says Ollie.

"Juniper, duck!" Galatea shouts. I duck just in time to avoid a sheep's gnashing jaws. It flies past my head and transforms in midair into a giant, flying sword. Specifically, the sword from my nightmares: *the one that stabs Kypris*. It's blazing gold and at least three times the size of a normal sword. It changes direction and zooms right at me—then spins sideways with a clang as Galatea blocks it with her own sword. Ollie reaches the edge of the quicksand, holding out the baseball bat for Sam to grab as a lifeline.

And suddenly, a voice cuts through everything:

WHEN THIRD EYE CLOSES, SHE IS LOST

THE ISLE OF KYPROS PAYS THE COST

I clutch at my head, gasping. "Who was that?"

"Who was what?" says Ollie.

"That voice!"

"Ollie, pull!" Sam grits out. He digs in his heels and pulls, with Sam clinging to the end of the bat. "June, grab on to me!" I wrap my arms around his waist and dig my heels into the grass. "Count of three! One, two, *heave*!"

We heave. The breath whooshes out of his lungs. With a noise like the world's biggest bathtub drain becoming unclogged, Sam's body erupts from the quicksand, and her momentum tosses all three of us into a tangled heap. I get a faceful of Ollie's bony shoulder and a mouthful of his hair. They roll off me, and my ribs expand.

"Look out!" Galatea tackles Sam out of the path of four deadly looking hooves. The flying sheep bleats angrily, releasing a gust of breath that smells like putrid garbage.

"Get inside the barn!" Galatea says, scrambling to her feet. "Go! I'm right behind you!" Her sword flashes. The sheep bursts into feathers and smoke.

We run around front to the barn doors, which are bolted with a padlock that some teenager has already done us the favor of unlocking. I fumble at it with shaky hands before yanking the doors open and practically falling inside. Galatea rounds the corner, the last three sheep flapping at her heels, and throws herself through the doors. We slam them shut behind her. *THUMP.* The doors rattle hard on their hinges. *THUMP. THUMP.* Then it's quiet. I slump back against the doors, heart pounding a drum solo. Freaking monster sheep.

"Guys?" says Ollie. "You might want to take a look at this."

With a distinct feeling of foreboding, I turn to look. Because we are in a barn, I'm sort of expecting to see the interior of a barn. You know, rafters and cobwebs and stuff. Instead, there are trees. And sunlight. And the floor beneath our feet is a carpet of moss.

We're not in a barn. We're in a forest.

12

We're surrounded by tall, thin trees. Tendrils of mist curl around the trunks, swirling in the shafts of sunlight that dapple the forest floor. Even the air is different, cool and misty, tinged with a sweetness that reminds me of honeysuckle.

"You guys are seeing this, too, right?" says Ollie.

"Uh-huh," Sam says faintly.

"Cool. Just checking."

"Quiet. Nobody move," Galatea says, and stalks forward with her sword raised. Sam, Ollie, and I hang back in a huddle as ordered. Ollie's white-knuckling his baseball bat. Sam's caked in mud from the waist down, eyes huge behind her glasses. I take slow, deep breaths, filling my lungs with the strangely sweet air. The door we came through has disappeared. There's no trace of the Old Barn.

"Is this because of the Crown of Horn?" I ask Galatea. "Did it take us somewhere?"

"I said *quiet*, Juniper."

I make a face at the back of her head.

"June, what's going on?" Ollie whispers.

Galatea whirls around. "Juniper. The voice you heard outside. What did it say?"

"Wh-what?"

"*What did it say?*"

"Um... 'When third eye closes, she is lost. The Isle of Kypros pays the cost.'"

"What else?" she demands.

"Nothing, that's it."

She swears loudly—at least I assume it's a swear, in Arkhean. It sure sounds like one.

"Sorry to interrupt, but can one of you maybe explain what's happening?" asks Ollie. "What is this place? Where are we?"

"I don't know," says Galatea.

"You don't know?" I blurt out.

"No! Of course I don't know! I don't understand any of this, Juniper! For all I'm aware, *all* the rotten old barns in your world have forests inside!" Her cheeks are flushed. "I assume, judging by your reactions, that they do not?"

"They do not," I confirm.

"Then *yes*, I suppose this forest must have something to do with the Crown of Horn, but I don't know how or why. Perhaps we haven't traveled anywhere. Perhaps this is a dream."

"It doesn't feel like a dream," says Sam, reaching down to pet the soft green moss on the forest floor. She rubs a yellow leaf between her fingers. "It feels real."

"I agree," says Galatea. "Just let me…think for a moment." She resumes stomping around the clearing, glowering off into the trees like she's expecting an answer to come barreling out of the shadows.

"All right, then," I mutter.

Ollie looks at me. "I have questions."

"It's…kind of a long story."

"Yeah," he says. "I figured it might be, considering, you know." He gestures at our surroundings. "Let's hear it."

"Yeah. Okay. Um…" Where do I even begin? Sam

and Ollie watch me expectantly. "You know how I said Galatea's visiting from Bulgaria?"

They nod.

"Yeah. So, that was a lie."

"You don't say," says Sam.

"Galatea's not from Bulgaria. She's the princess of this place called the Isle of Kypros. And the thing about the Isle of Kypros is that it doesn't exist on Earth. I know it sounds nuts, but I swear it's the truth. Galatea came here from a different world."

"Oh, like from another planet? Or is it more like a parallel- or alternate-universe situation?" asks Sam.

I blink at her. "Uh..."

"That's fine. We can come back to that," she says. "Go on."

"...Okay, so, the thing is, she didn't mean to come here. She was trying to go somewhere else, using this magical object called the Crown of Horn, which was supposed to take her straight to, um, the Isle of Dreams. That's where this god lives. Dreamtender. That's the long story—I'll get to that in a sec. But the crown malfunctioned some-how, and she ended up here, and somewhere in there, the crown disappeared. It was gone when she showed up in my room. Now we're trying to find it, because it's her only way home."

"How does the Crown of Horn work?" asks Sam.

"Oh, I can actually explain this! It's made of the same stuff as this magical gate on the Isle of Dreams. So it works the same as the gate. It transports you on and off the island. Or it's supposed to, anyway."

"I see. And what was that about the god?" she says.

"Dreamtender, the god of dreams. She's got a grudge against Skyrender, who's like the king of gods, and we think maybe she's planning to hurt the goddess of Galatea's island to get revenge on him?"

"I'm gonna need a flowchart," says Ollie.

"I'll make one," says Sam.

"But let me get this straight." Ollie points at Galatea, who is busy examining a tree trunk. "She is the princess of an island in another world, and she was trying to go fight an angry god but accidentally opened an interdimensional portal to small-town South Florida, of all places, and now she's stuck here unless you guys find a magic crown. And also there's like five other gods involved somehow."

"Only three, but yeah," I say. "That's pretty much it. Oh. Her island floats in the sky. And it's disappearing."

"Sorry, what?" says Ollie.

"Yeah, it's literally turning into smoke."

"And this island floats in..."

"The sky. You know, where birds live."

"Got it," he says. "Okay. Anything else?"

I think for a moment. "We came out here to the Old Barn because we think Sam's meteor is actually the Crown of Horn."

"Ha!" Sam smacks a fist in her hand. "I knew it wasn't a regular meteor!"

I can't help but look back and forth between them. "So, you guys just...believe me?"

"It makes a lot more sense than Bulgaria," Sam says.

"Does it?" I ask.

She raises her voice. "Galatea, who is the current president of Bulgaria?"

Silence.

"You guys are not masterminds," she says, then shrugs. "I might've had more trouble believing you if we hadn't just been attacked by flying sheep and were not currently standing in a forest that's supposed to be a barn. Frankly, if it weren't magic, I'd be worried. Well, *more* worried."

"Speaking of flying sheep: Why?" says Ollie.

"Good question," I say. "That's a Galatea question. I have no idea."

Galatea rejoins us at that moment. "Oneiroi," she says. "Those things were oneiroi—dream spirits. They act as messengers of the god of dreams. Their natural form is that of black birds, but they can take the form of dreams or nightmares. I don't suppose any of you have nightmares about, ah, sheep?"

Ollie raises his hand.

Sam looks at him. "Really?"

"I got bit by a sheep at a petting zoo when I was five. So, now I have recurring nightmares about being slowly devoured by a hoard of fanged, flesh-eating sheep."

"Holy god, Oliver," says Sam.

"I know, it's my trauma."

"And the quicksand?" says Galatea.

Sam nods. "That was me. Last week, I had this nightmare where I flunked a test because I got stuck in quicksand on the way to school and didn't get there in time."

"I feel like getting stuck in quicksand should be a valid excuse," says Ollie.

"Right? But in the nightmare, Mr. Henries was just like, 'Do you expect me to believe you got stuck in quicksand?' I was so mad."

"And the sword," says Galatea. "Juniper, I expect that was you?"

"Yeah. It's the one from the dream."

"Godkiller," she says gravely. "The fabled sword, one of the few weapons capable of spilling divine blood—of taking an immortal life. No one knows if it's real. The stories claim it was created so mortals could defend themselves against the gods."

I frown. "If the oneiroi were sent by Dreamtender, then that voice I heard…"

Galatea nods. "It must have been her. The message was phrased like part of a prophecy. And I believe I know what it means." A vein ticks in her jaw. "*When third eye closes*—I believe that's a reference to an event known in my world as the Triple Eclipse. Once every hundred years, the three moons are eclipsed at the same time. There are many names for it: the Night of Hollows, the Closing of the Eyes.

On this night, the gods temporarily lose their divine powers. My people spend the night in worship, gathering in temples, burning food and wine, and praying without rest to help the gods retain their strength until morning."

I have a sinking feeling about this. "When was the last Triple Eclipse?"

"One hundred years ago."

"Right. So the next one is..."

"Two nights from now."

Of course it is. "And the prophecy?"

"*When third eye closes, she is lost. The Isle of Kypros pays the cost.* I'm not sure it could get much clearer than that," Galatea says grimly. "When the moons go dark, something terrible will happen to Kypris. And my island will probably disappear entirely, and forever. It certainly seems to align with the second part of the Oracle's prophecy." She recounts the prophecy to Sam and Ollie: "*To rightful owner must return the stolen crown, or all will burn.*" Then she lets out a breath, steeling herself. "However, that's something to worry about later. For now, let's focus on finding our way out of this forest."

"Then, you think there's a way out?" I ask.

She nods. "In fact, I don't think we've truly *gone*

anywhere. I think it's more like a *somewhere* has sprung up around us. This isn't a dream, but nor is it entirely real. It is made of a magic so powerful it can only come from one source. I believe the Crown of Horn lies at the heart of this forest, and I'm going to find it." She looks at us. "You three should remain here until I return."

"Nope," I say.

"Juniper," she says. "I'll leave my sword with you."

"Double nope. Even more nope. I don't know how to use a sword."

"I really don't think we should split up," Sam adds.

"Yeah. Look what the oneiroi did to my baseball bat," says Ollie, showcasing the gnarly tooth marks all over the end. "I don't think it'll survive another attack."

"Why do you have a baseball bat, anyway? Weren't you guys just looking for a meteor?" I ask.

"Yeah, but the Old Barn gives me the creeps," says Ollie.

"We take precautions," says Sam.

"Oh, nice." I turn back to Galatea. "Anyway, no way you're ditching us here to go off on your own. What if something attacks us? What if something attacks you?"

"I will fight it with my fists."

"What? That's a terrible answer. What if it's a bear? Are you gonna fight a bear with your fists?"

"Why would I be attacked by a bear?"

"I don't know! We're in the woods! Magic woods! Magic bear!"

"I'm not going to be attacked by a bear."

"You literally don't know that."

"Are we going to be attacked by a bear?" says Ollie.

"No," says Galatea, then: "Well..."

"All right, that's settled," says Sam. "We're not splitting up. That's how people die in horror movies."

"Seconded," I say.

"Thirded," says Ollie.

I turn to Galatea. "You're officially outnumbered. Welcome to democracy, Princess."

She rolls her eyes. "Fine. But stay behind me, and keep your eyes and ears open."

Ollie tightens his grip on the baseball bat.

"Lead the way," I tell Galatea, and we start off into the forest.

13

For a few minutes, we walk in a wary silence. The forest is sunlit, full of rough-barked trees and carpeted with moss, fallen leaves, and pine needles. Songbirds dart overhead, fluting their songs. I don't see any black-winged oneiroi, or any other animals, for that matter. The canopy is too thick to see the sun, just tiny chips of sky, so it's hard to tell which direction we're going. (Sam tries the compass app on her phone, which is how we discover our phones are dead, which, to be frank, doesn't feel promising.)

Galatea stops. "Do you hear that?"

There's a new sound under the birdsong, light and tinkling like water, or tiny bells.

"It sounds like... But it can't be," she breathes.

Then she breaks into a run, crashing off into the trees. I exchange startled looks with the others and give chase. We catch up to Galatea at the edge of a clearing. This time I actually do collide with her. She pitches forward, arms pinwheeling, before righting herself. "Thundering skies, Juniper!"

"Sorry, sorry!"

It's a good thing she didn't fall. She's led us to the edge of a forest pool. The water is deep and clear, ringed by the tangled roots of a tree. The tree has silvery bark and a beautiful pink-and-white-flowering crown. I can see cherries among the flowers, dark ripe jumbles. It's clear we've found the source of the noise. The cherries are all trembling, shivering of their own accord, creating a sound like a chorus of high, gently chiming bells.

"I can't believe it," Galatea says. "A singing cherry."

"What's a singing cherry?" asks Sam.

"They grow only in the orchards of Kypros. In spring and summer, as the fruits ripen, you can hear the sound of bells from one end of the island to the other.... Or so I'm told. The singing cherries haven't bloomed since before I was born. I've heard them before, but only in my dreams."

She picks her way over to the tree, hardly taking her eyes off it as she navigates the slippery roots surrounding the pool. "I've had singing cherry wine, stewed singing cherries, singing cherry jam, but never the fresh fruits. They're meant to taste of honey and sunlight."

Her face tilts up, briefly golden, then dappled in shadow. I glance at her reflection in the pool and do a double take. It looks like her reflection is wearing a crown. Then I realize the pale shape I'm seeing in the water isn't part of her reflection at all.

"Galatea. Look in the water," I say.

She ignores me, turning in a slow circle beneath the branches.

"Galatea, look! There's something at the bottom of the pool."

"That white thing?" asks Ollie.

"Yeah. What's that look like to you?" I say.

"Not sure." He moves closer to the edge of the pool. "Yo, Princess Galatea. Check this out."

She's fixated on the cherries. "They look perfectly ripe."

"I don't think you should eat that," Sam says suddenly. "Isn't there a thing about...eating the food in dreams? Or something?"

"I think that's the fairy realm," says Ollie.

"Still," she says. "If this type of tree only grows on the Isle of Kypros, then how is one here? What if it's something else? I really don't think we should go around eating unidentified fruits. Just, in general. As a life rule."

"Yeah, agreed," I say. "Please don't eat that."

Galatea doesn't seem to hear us. Meanwhile, Ollie's leaning farther over the water. "Whatever's down there is partly buried," he says. "If I can just poke it a little..."

He dips the bat into the water.

The sound of bells cuts off. Then there's an ominous CREEEEEEAK. All of a sudden, the tree seems to have a mind of its own. Its silver trunk twists like a spine. Its branches start waving in the air. Hairy roots shoot out of the pool to wrap around Galatea's ankles, yanking her to the ground. She cries out in pain.

Something hits me on the arm. "Ow!" I yelp, and it happens again, something small hitting me hard on the shoulder. The tree is pelting us with cherries. Sam, Ollie, and I cover our heads with our hands, trying not to get hit in the face. It's like a rain of BB gun pellets—each hit *stings*. Galatea's still struggling to free herself from the tree roots, hacking uselessly at them with her sword.

"The water!" she grunts. "The thing in the water!"

"Oh, *now* you're paying attention!" I shout, but scramble to the pool's edge. I can see the pale thing glinting at the bottom, half-buried in sand. The water's so clear, I can't tell how deep it is. It could be four feet or fifteen.

CREEEEEEEAK. A branch swoops through the air, nearly knocking Ollie right off his feet. There's no time to waste. I suck in a breath and jump into the forest pool. Cool water closes over my head, making my ears pop. The pool is definitely deeper than it looked from the surface. I squint through the blurry water, searching for a bit of white. *There.* Kicking hard, I dive down to the sandy bottom, fingers closing around a smooth, curving object.

A green mountainside—

A mossy statue, face turned to the sky—

I gasp reflexively, which is a super-bad idea when you're underwater. Choking, coughing out streams of bubbles, I push off the bottom of the pool and break the surface, simultaneously hacking up water and gasping for breath. A hand wraps around my arm, and there's Ollie, pulling me out of the water.

The first thing I notice is the tree has stopped viciously attacking us. It's gone still again, no longer hurling cherries.

Then, as we watch, the world…dissolves. The forest around us, the trees and green canopy and songbirds, the pool, the singing cherry—it all fades away into swirls of smoke. And we're not standing in a forest anymore. We're in the Old Barn. Sunlight pokes through worn-out holes in the tin roof, shining on dusty old floorboards strewn with litter. The walls are covered in graffiti. There's a puddle of rainwater on the floor at my feet. I'm racked with another cough, doubling over—but still clutching the crown.

"Outside," Galatea says. "Fresh air."

We pile out into the afternoon sunlight, where I take a couple of deep breaths. Then I hold up the Crown of Horn, triumphant, so Galatea can see. "Worth it," I wheeze. "Totally worth it."

She stares. "Juniper," she says, an odd note in her voice. "Where's the rest?"

"What?" I look at the crown.

But it's not a crown. It's a single shard of horn, like a broken rib.

My mouth drops open. "No, this was—this was it."

"Where's the *rest*?"

"This is all there was."

Galatea's eyes go very wide, fixed in horror on the broken crown.

I scramble to reassure her. "I'm—I'm sure the rest is... here. Somewhere. Somewhere around...this place."

She presses a hand to her mouth.

"The meteor!" Sam says. "The meteor broke apart in midair, remember? I was watching—I saw the whole thing. There were three burning trails, like fragments falling to Earth."

Fragments. Shattered pieces. My heart sinks.

"O-okay," I say, trying to hide my fear. What if it's broken beyond repair? "Um, we just have to find the other fragments. That's not so bad, especially if there's only three. We've already got one. So, one down, two to go. Right, Galatea?"

She nods mutely.

Sam takes out her phone. "Let's meet up tomorrow morning. I'll check over the data I recorded last night. I might be able to figure out where the other fragments landed, or at least the general areas we should search."

"Wait. Are you sure?" I ask. "I mean, you guys don't have to get mixed up in this."

She gives me an incredulous look. "June. We came out here today to search for bits of a comet. Lumps of smoldering space rock. Instead, we learn there's a whole other world with gods and magic and *interdimensional portals*, and I'm supposed to just, what? Go home and study my vocab words? I don't think so. This is the most fascinating thing that's ever happened in this town. I want in."

Ollie nods. "I go where she goes. Also, yeah. This is a lot more interesting than tossing rocks in the swamp to watch them go splash."

"I'll make a group chat," Sam says.

We exchange phone numbers. My phone buzzes twice. We say our goodbyes and part ways, Sam and Ollie having come out here from a different direction. Then it's just me and Galatea walking back to where I left my bike, Galatea trailing miserably behind.

"Um," I say, "are you okay carrying the—the crown? While you're in the basket?"

"Yes. I'd like to carry it."

"Okay."

I hop onto the seat. Galatea situates herself carefully, clutching the crown piece. I feel awful. Her only hope of ever returning home, of saving her kingdom, is broken, maybe destroyed. I know it's not my fault, but it kind of feels like it. After all, I'm the one who pulled it out of the water. I'm the one who drew her obsessively, who wished for her to be here, in this world.

It's funny. I spent most of today wishing she'd say a bit less. Now that she's silent, I wish she'd say something. Even something snooty or bossy. She doesn't. So I don't, either. We bike all the way home without a word.

14

Predictably, Mom is overjoyed to meet my shiny new friend Galatea, who she thinks I met at Noah's house. She asks a million questions about life in Bulgaria, and Galatea does a generally okay job at answering in ways that don't make her sound bananas. I have to jump in a few times.

"When she says dragon pipes, what she means is, uh, bagpipes," I say (honestly, she won't quit with the freaking dragons), and Mom's eyes go round.

"You play the *bagpipes*?" she says.

"Oh yes," says Galatea. Mom's fawning seems to have

cheered her up a bit after the discovery of the broken crown. "Quite well."

"I tried to get Junebug into playing guitar—how cool would that be!—but she was terrible," Mom says. "Poor kid can't carry a tune in a bucket."

"Mom," I complain.

"Her dad plays harmonica. I'll have him—oh! It's past six! Dinner!" She flies into action. We've been sitting at the kitchen counter to chat, sipping iced tea. So far, it's going well. Mom happily believed that Galatea already asked her parents if she could sleep over and that there was no need for a phone call because they only speak Bulgarian. ("Just tell them the Harveys say hello and welcome!" she said.) Now she pulls out a box of pasta and starts rummaging in the fridge. "Okay, girls. You're on veggie-chopping duty."

Dad comes into the kitchen a few minutes later. He squints and puts on his glasses when he sees Galatea. "Whoa! I knew I was seeing more kids than usual in here."

"Dad," I complain.

He smiles and sticks out his hand. "I'm Rob, June's dad."

"Galatea." She eyes his hand curiously. I mime a

handshake behind Dad's back, and she reaches out and shakes it. "It is an honor to meet you."

"The manners on this one," Mom says. "June, why don't you talk like that?"

"I wasn't raised right," I reply, and rinse off another zucchini.

Dad puts on some music—the twangy bluegrass stuff he likes—in the living room and turns it up loud enough that we can hear. He sets to work at the stove, stir-frying the chopped zucchini and bell peppers, which I'm personally very grateful for. I don't want Galatea's first experience of my family's home cooking to involve cinnamon-lemon-nutmeg veggie stir-fry.

I've missed this, I realize. Cooking with Mom and Dad. Some of my favorite memories are of sitting on the back porch of our old house, shucking corn into a paper grocery bag, picking off all the silky hairs while Dad talked about one thing or another or we listened to Mom singing Dolly Parton in the kitchen, her voice carrying out through the screen door. Since we moved and Dad got busier, we've all seen one another a lot less.

Galatea steals the last couple of garlic cloves off my cutting board. "Hey," I say mildly, before realizing she's finished chopping everything else. Not only that, but her slices are way neater than mine. "Do you cook a lot?" I ask. It's not what I would've expected from a princess, but to be fair, I've never actually met a princess before.

"No," she says, and proceeds to mince the garlic like a pro. She's better at it than Dad, even. It takes her like two seconds.

I lower my voice. "Is it because of your sword-fighting skills?"

She looks amused. "No, Juniper. That's not how swords work."

"Then how are you so good at this?"

"Practice," she says, and quickly busies herself bringing the cutting board over to Dad. She sticks near the stove, watching him.

"You just said you don't cook," I mumble, but let it go.

Mom's singing along to the music as she stirs the pasta. She's got a pretty good voice, all high and clear. I start in washing the sharp knives, and Galatea joins me at the sink. After a minute, she says, "Your mother was right."

"Hmm?"

"You can't carry a tune."

I feel my ears turn bright red. I was definitely singing a

little under my breath. "Shut up," I say, and flick water at her. "I'd like to see you try."

"Well, yes. I'm a naturally gifted singer."

That gets my attention. "Wait, for real?"

"Of course," she says. "It's the sea nymph blood. My voice could bring down the heavens—that's what everyone says."

"Okay, I mean, now you have to sing something," I tell her. "Like, you can't just say that and then not sing something."

She glances at my parents, who are busy chatting at the stove. "All right," she says. "If you insist." She closes her eyes. I wait in breathless anticipation. Of course she's an amazing singer—like the Little Mermaid or something. She's probably amazing at everything she does, always.

Galatea opens her eyes and begins to sing.

She lasts about five seconds before bursting into laughter at the look on my face. "Oh my god," I say. "Was that for real? Was that your real voice?"

"Yes," she wheezes. "Yes, it was."

"Oh my god." I stare at her in amazement—though admittedly not the kind I was expecting. "Oh my god, you're worse than I am." She cackles. "That was so bad.

I don't even know that song, but I know that's not how it sounds."

"I can't sing at all," she says gleefully. "You really believed me, though."

"Uh, yeah, I thought I was about to hear a beautiful sea nymph song. Like, the most beautiful thing ever. You said you were naturally gifted."

"Ah," she says, "but I didn't say it was a *good* gift."

After dinner, we watch a movie in the living room with Mom and Dad. It's an animated movie I haven't seen before, and I usually love animation, but tonight I don't absorb a single frame. I spend the whole time watching Galatea, who is absolutely enraptured by the screen. Light and color flickers over her face, her huge eyes. When it's over and the screen goes black, she lets out a sigh that seems to come from the depths of her. She doesn't move, even as my parents get up to put away the empty pop-corn bowl. Finally, I nudge her ankle with my foot. "You good?" I ask.

"Mm-hmm," she says.

Saying good night to my parents, we retreat to my room. I set up a sleeping bag for Galatea. "Do you mind the floor?" I ask. "You can take the bed if you want. I can change the sheets."

"I'd quite like to sleep on the floor," she says, giving the lumpy purple sleeping bag a look of interest. "I've never done so before. It feels rather adventurous."

"Cool. All yours."

We take turns in the bathroom. I lend her a toothbrush, plus a baggy T-shirt and a pair of pajama shorts. Then we settle into bed. I watch her tuck the crown piece under her pillow; then I turn off the light. I roll onto my back, looking up at the glow-in-the-dark stars the kid who lived here before me left behind. Most of them don't actually glow anymore, but they're also pretty much fused to the ceiling, so they stay.

It's quiet for a long moment. I listen to the misty rain outside.

"I like your parents," Galatea whispers.

I blink. "Yeah?"

"Yes. They're very kind."

"Yeah, they are." I'm trying to puzzle out the tone of

her voice. "Is your dad...?" I don't know how to finish the question.

"Mm," she says. "My father's amazing. He's a hero. A king beloved by all. I...I miss him very much."

"When's he coming back?"

"Oh, soon. Very soon."

"Hey," I say. "Maybe by the time he gets back, we'll have solved this thing. You know. Saved the island ourselves."

"I hope so," she whispers.

"Sorry you miss him," I say, rolling onto my side. It's too dark to see her. All I can make out is a tangle of dark hair on the pillow. I think she's hiding her face in the sleeping bag, which explains why she sounds a bit muffled. "I know the feeling. I mean, kind of. I've missed my dad lately, too." I start to feel silly. "I mean, he hasn't gone anywhere. I know it's not the same. But...yeah. I miss him sometimes."

She doesn't answer for a while. "It's lonely," she says at last.

"Yeah," I say. "I know that a bit, too."

"Yeah?"

I let out a breath. "Today at school, that was the first time

I've had lunch in the cafeteria—like with other people— since I started there. If Sam hadn't invited us, or you hadn't been there, I would've eaten alone in the library. That's what I've been doing all month."

"Why?" she asks.

"I don't know. I'm just—I'm not good at that kind of thing."

"Not good at what kind of thing?"

I wince. "Making friends."

"Hmm." The sleeping bag rustles as she shifts. "I think you're all right."

I press a hand to my chest under the covers. It feels like my heart's glowing.

"Do you think we'll share dreams tonight?" Galatea asks.

"Oh. I don't know," I say. "I guess we'll find out."

"Mm."

"Do you—do you want to?"

"Want to what?"

"Share dreams."

She sniffs. "Do *you* want to?"

"I asked first."

"I'm a princess."

"Not of here, not of me, and also I don't care."

It sounds like she muffles a snort in her pillow. "Well, then," she says. "I suppose we'll find out. Good night, Juniper."

"Night, Galatea."

I roll onto my back again, gaze finding the two glow-in-the-dark stars that still faintly light up. On the nights I can't sleep, I make up stories about them, these two stars at the end of the universe.

If Galatea and I were stars instead of people and spoke in light instead of words, I'd tell her, *I want to see you in my dreams.* If I could make her understand that star-sized, hot, bright thought without having to voice it aloud, that would be so much easier. Because it's too big for words. It's so big, it can't fit in my chest or my mouth or this room or this world. It's so big, it could illuminate a corner of the universe all on its own. And what am I supposed to do with that?

In the end, I'm too shy to say anything else, just in case I'm the only one lying here with a star lodged in my throat. And maybe I am, because Galatea doesn't say anything, either, and before long her breaths slow into the rhythm of sleep.

In the dream, I'm riding on the back of a giant black bird, and by *riding* I mean *clinging on to for dear life*. Fingers twisted in the bird's feathers, I lean low over its neck as we soar through dark, stormy clouds. Thunder crashes all around us, and lightning arcs up ahead, illuminating the cloud bellies. Wind and rain lash at my face. The bird dives suddenly, and we pop out of the cloud layer like a cork, into the open air above a green valley ringed with mountains. The rain drenches me instantly, and it becomes that much harder to hang on to the bird's slick feathers. I think I left my stomach about fifty feet up.

The bird tips sideways, adjusting to the wind, and I can see more details of the land below. It must be the Isle of Kypros, because—well, it's an island in the sky. From my bird's-eye view, I can see the valley and mountains on one end of the island and on the other, past the mountains, rolling hills and a city that looks like a handful of seashells, a pale jumble glittering in the storm light.

Thunder booms so loud my teeth rattle. Then something—no, some*one*—falls out of the clouds. A bolt of lightning snakes down to strike them in midair. For a moment, they're a bright dot in the storm, but I'm too far away to make out any details. The lightning fades, and they're falling, and I lose sight of them long before they hit the ground.

The bird keeps flying. I see a glimmer in the rain up ahead. As we get closer, it resolves into the outline of a doorway, or a gate, made of pale fire and just hovering there in the sky. There doesn't seem to be anything on the other side except more storm clouds, but the bird flies directly toward it. We pass through the gate—and into somewhere entirely new. The storm and the island are gone. Now we're flying low over an ocean shoreline, all sand and rocks and rolling waves. The bird's head dips, and I hang on tight as it flies down to land among the sharp rocks at the base of a cliff.

"Juniper?"

I slide off the bird's back, dropping a couple of feet into the cold water. "Galatea?"

"Juniper! Over here!"

She's standing in the surf a little farther out, water lapping at her thighs. When I splash over to her, I can see she's turned to ivory from the waist down. White tendrils are creeping slowly up her arms and over her chiton. She looks me in the eye and says:

FLAME TO ASH AND FLESH TO BONE

WHAT WAS REAPED MUST NOW BE SOWN

Her mouth forms the words, but that's not her voice.

"Dreamtender," I say.

Galatea frowns, and her familiar voice returns. "You have to help me. The water's rising, and I can't move."

"You didn't hear her?"

"Hear who? Juniper, come on. The tide's coming in."

She's right. The water's up to our shoulders now, rising faster than the ivory can cover Galatea's body. At this rate, the water will reach her nose and mouth before the ivory does.

"The tide's coming in," she says again.

Cold water laps against the underside of my chin.

"Juniper, the *tide's*—"

The water swallows her voice, the sea closes above our heads, and—

15

I jolt awake to sunlight.

My bedroom is champagne gold and sparkling with dust motes like, I'm in the bottom of a glass on New Year's. I check the clock—it's eight thirty AM. I poke my head off the edge of the bed to find Galatea already awake and looking expectantly at me.

"What did you see?" she asks.

I tell her about the first part of the dream: the bird, the storm, the figure falling out of the sky, the burning gate. "The gate transported us to the beach where I found you. And then you looked at me and spoke in Dreamtender's voice. Do you remember that?"

"No," she says with a frown. "I remember everything else—you and the water—but not that. What did I say?"

"'Flame to ash and flesh to bone, what was reaped must now be sown.'"

Her frown deepens into a scowl. "She's playing with us," she says. "Feeding us a prophecy line by line, just to watch us squirm as we try to riddle it out. What do we have so far...? *When third eye closes, she is lost. The Isle of Kypros pays the cost. Flame to ash and flesh to bone, what was reaped must now be sown....*"

We ponder for a moment. "*Flesh to bone* sounds like what happens to you in the dreams," I say. "I don't know about *flame to ash*. Divine flame, maybe?"

"*What was reaped must now be sown*," she mutters. "Reap what you sow....What was reaped...? Gods-all, that could refer to anything!"

"It's a bit vague," I agree.

"And what of the person who fell from the sky? Do you think it was Kypris? Was it another of Dreamtender's threats?"

I shake my head, clueless. "I was too far away to tell."

Galatea shoves her face into the pillow and lets out a muffled groan. Just then my phone buzzes with a message from the group chat with Sam and Ollie.

Sam

Hey good morning

I have a theory about where to look for the next pieces of the crown.

Come to my house? It's easier to explain in person.

Also my parents are out for the morning.

So no questions ☺ lol

Also, if possible, pls bring rubber boots.

Ollie

on my way

Me

!!!!!!

holy crow

yeah be there asap

whats your address?

Ten minutes later, Galatea is once again perched in the basket of my bike and I'm pedaling down Sam's street. Turns out she lives super close by, only a few blocks from my house. (I asked Mom if Galatea and I could go hang out with my other new friends, and she was predictably thrilled. Sometimes being chronically lonely and awkward has its perks.)

Leaving my bike near Sam's mailbox, Galatea and I go up to knock on the front door. My hair's sticking to my temples with sweat. "Bowser," we hear from inside, along with the sound of furious pawing. "You're in the way!"

It takes Sam two tries to get the door open. That's something Texas and Florida have in common: Wooden doors swell in the heat, get stuck in the doorframes.

"Come on in," she says at last, blocking a panting, friendly looking border collie from attacking us with kisses. "This is Bowser. He doesn't know how to behave."

Sam leads us through the house and out to the back-yard, where there's a white dome the size of a garden shed sitting on the grass.

"Welcome to the Sky Pod," she says, tossing a smile over her shoulder. "Glad you could make it."

"For sure," I say, a little wide-eyed.

The inside of the Sky Pod is mostly taken up by a big telescope on a tripod, but there's enough floor space for the three of us to sit. Ollie shows up a couple of minutes later, and we scoot over to make room. My bare knee brushes Galatea's.

"I bet you're wondering why I've gathered you all here today," says Sam. "Wow. I've always wanted to say that. Anyway." She lays a piece of paper on the floor between us. It's a printed-out satellite map of Cypress, showing an aerial view of the town and neighborhoods surrounded by wild green. "I did some thinking last night. First, I looked over the photos I took two nights ago—you know, when I saw that 'meteor' that turned out to be Galatea's crown. I wanted to see if I could triangulate a general radius where the pieces might have landed around town based on the crown's exact positioning and distance from the earth's surface when it broke apart in midair, plus the angle of descent for the falling debris."

She looks up, waiting for us to comment.

"Yes," I volunteer, successfully hiding the fact that I have no clue what she just said.

"Right. So, I was comparing the photos to a map of Cypress when I realized something." She marks two dots on the map with a red marker. "This is the Old Barn," she says, indicating one. "And over here is June's house."

"...How do you know where I live?"

"How often do you think people move to this town?" she says. "I googled recent house sales in the area. Took five seconds. Fourteen Hyacinth Street, right?" I nod. "Right. So anyway, as we know, these two spots are the locations where extradimensional events have occurred. Magical hot spots, if you will. Galatea first appeared at June's house, and we found a piece of the crown at the Old Barn. Right?" We all nod. "Now, check this out." Sam takes out a ruler and draws two intersecting lines so the map's divided into four equal boxes. Each line originates from one of the dots. She labels the ends of the lines with N, E, S, and W, with north being the Old Barn and west being my house. Then she circles the spot in the center where the lines cross. "Guess what this building is."

"Bowling alley," says Ollie.

"Monster battle arena," says Galatea.

"Disney World," I say.

"So, Disney World is not in Cypress," says Sam. "Disney World is not anywhere near Cypress. If it was, a lot more people would live here. We'd probably have more than one movie theater."

"I couldn't think of another Florida landmark," I explain. "Galatea's the one who said monster battle arena."

Galatea sticks her nose in the air. "It was a *guess.*"

"To be fair," says Ollie, "if there was a monster battle arena anywhere in this world, it would be in Florida. And it would involve alligators."

"Alligators?" Galatea asks.

"Giant swamp lizards," he says.

"Giant—!" Galatea shoots me an incredulous look. "So, when I mention dragons at the lunch table, I get kicked in the ankle, yet you do, in fact, have giant lizards wandering around?"

"Okay, gators and dragons are not the same thing," I say.

"How would you know? They certainly sound—"

Sam coughs loudly. "*Anyway,*" she says, drawing our attention back to the map, "this spot in the center? This rectangular building? That's Franklin B. Pruitt. Turns out the Old Barn and June's house are both exactly two miles from the middle school in different cardinal directions: north and west. Here's my theory: I think maybe the school is some sort of…focal point. You know, like the center of a circle."

Galatea leans forward, excited. "I sensed a trace of magic at the school!" she says. "In the art room! It was quite faint—not nearly as potent as it was at the Old Barn—but I could sense it, remember, Juniper?"

"Yeah." I keep my eyes firmly on the map. Oh, I remember. I remember hiding in the art room during the dance. I remember crying alone in the dark, drawing her, feeling that insistent tug in my belly. I remember whispering to her: *Why are you in my head?*

I point at the ends of the south and east lines. "Um, if the school is the focal point, does that mean we should look for the crown pieces here?"

"That's what I think," Sam says. "It's just a guess, but unless I'm mistaken, that's all we've got. I already looked up the locations. Exactly two miles south of the school, there's this place called Cypress Auto Salvage, which comes up online as a junkyard." She draws a dot on a lone building at the bottom edge of the map. "Exactly two miles east of the school is…well…a random spot way out in the swamp."

The final dot goes in the middle of a thick, dark fur of trees.

"So thaaaat's why you said to bring rubber boots," Ollie says.

Sam smiles grimly. "We're going off road."

16

The swamp is smelly, both in the sense of being stinky and in the sense of just plain having a lot of smells: hot river water, mud and mildew, rotten eggs, and the almost-sweet scent of decaying leaves. At first the water is only a couple of inches high, but as we venture farther into the shadows of the cypress trees, it gets deeper and deeper. Mud sucks at our boots with every step. I kind of thought swamps were supposed to look like big mud puddles, but this one looks like a flooded forest.

Sam's in the lead with her phone GPS. "I have so many questions, I don't know where to begin," she says, splashing purposefully through the muck. "About magic, about this other world, about the crown—like, how does the crown work? I know it's magic, but how does that magic function? Galatea came here, to Earth, to *Florida*, from another planet or a parallel universe or something, and that means she had to cross the universe—she *crossed the universe*—to get here, but how? Did she come through a wormhole?"

"A what?" says Galatea.

"A wormhole. It's like...Here." She stops to fish the map of Cypress out of her pocket, unfolding it to show us. "Ignore the map. Just pretend this piece of paper is the universe. These two points"—she indicates the north and south dots—"are far away from each other, right? So, let's say you're trying to get from one point to the other. You'd think the easiest way would be to travel in a straight line." She traces a fingertip along the red line she drew earlier, connecting the dots. "But what if there was a shortcut?" She bends the paper so the two points are touching. "That's a wormhole. Maybe Galatea came through one, which— well, it could mean our worlds are connected somehow. I mean, why *here*, you know? Why now?"

"I hear something," Galatea says suddenly. "Get behind me."

She draws her sword. We duck behind her, scanning the trees for any sign of movement, braced for an attack. "Oneiroi?" I ask in a whisper.

"Not sure."

Ollie raises his chewed-up baseball bat.

We hear wingbeats. A moment later, the air is a riot of flapping wings and feathers as hundreds of birds pour out of the sky to settle in the branches above us. They don't resemble giant black-winged oneiroi, but they're definitely not your average flock. No two birds are the same kind. I spot sparrows and starlings, woodpeckers, owls, sharp-eyed hawks and bright little songbirds, all sharing the same branches with complete disregard for the food chain. Ducks and geese land in the water with a series of splashes; then the big, old wetland kings arrive one by one: white crane, egret, heron, their wingspans nearly clipping the trees. All the birds settle and go still, just...watching us.

"Okay, whose nightmare is this?" Ollie asks.

The four of us exchange blank looks. "Maybe they're not oneiroi," says Galatea. "Maybe this is more like the forest in the Old Barn—a living dream." She presses her fingers to her forehead. "I can sense potent magic here, but I don't think it's coming from the birds."

Sam lights up. "We must be close to the crown... piece...." She trails off, eyes going huge. I turn to see what she's looking at, and my stomach *drops*. An enormous alligator is slicing through the water, heading straight toward us. And I mean this thing is the size of a pickup truck. If this gator got onto a golf course, it would make the news. It comes to a stop a few feet away; it's so long that half its body is still among the trees. Strangely, the birds don't react to its arrival, not even the ones in chomping distance. The gator swims off to the side, tail smacking the water, and stops again. It looks back at us. It...nods.

"Am I nuts, or does it want us to follow?" I ask.

"I vote we do what the nice alligator wants," says Ollie.

"What if what it wants is to eat us?"

Galatea hefts her sword. "I can handle an overgrown lizard, Juniper. You were right—they're nothing like dragons."

So, we follow the gator deeper into the swamp. The birds stay behind—except for one, the white crane, who takes an elegant step onto the gator's bumpy back and is carried as smoothly as a ferryman in a riverboat. Our phones go dead at some point, just like the forest, but the old-school compass Sam brought confirms we're headed due south.

Soon more animals come slinking out of the shadows. Snakes, turtles, and frogs trail behind us in the water; squirrels chase one another in the branches overhead. I spot a few deer following us at a distance, their bodies soft brown and mottled with watery light. Dragonflies dip to kiss the water. And I guess it wouldn't be Florida if our magical entourage didn't include clouds of mosquitoes.

"Eugh." Galatea flicks yet another one off her arm. "Tell me why this world is trying to drink my blood."

"My mom says if mosquitoes really like you, it means your blood is sweet." I do not know why I say this.

"My blood is divine."

"Not divine enough to repel mosquitoes."

"*Eugh*," she says. "I can't wait to leave this place."

That shuts me up.

After a few more minutes of slogging through shin-deep water and slapping away mosquitoes, a large, dark shape comes into view up ahead. It looks like a pile of mud. The gator's leading us toward it. Suddenly, the crane leaps into the air and glides to land on the mud pile, feathers fanning out like brushstrokes. With a splash of its mighty tail, our guide gator swims off into the trees, too fast to follow. The other animals seem to take this as a signal, and all except the crane fly, swim, and scamper away at once, until the swamp is eerily still.

"That's not ominous," Ollie mutters.

Sticking close, the four of us approach the strange mound. I don't know about the others, but I'm half expecting it to attack at any moment. After all, the singing cherry tree fought tooth and nail (uh, root and branch?) to keep its piece of the crown, nearly crushing Galatea and drowning me in the process. So far, it seems like whatever gets a taste of the crown's magic will want to hold on to it.

The mud pile is caked with leaves and bits of litter: empty bottles and fast-food wrappers, a moldy old shoe. The white crane regards us silently from its perch at the top.

"That's my favorite constellation," Sam murmurs. "The Crane."

"We have a crane constellation as well," Galatea says, wading a bit closer to the mound. "In the northern skies. My father used to—"

She cuts off when the mound emits a low, rumbling growl. The four of us scramble back as the whole thing shudders and quakes like a volcano on the brink of eruption, sending waves of swamp water rippling out.

"Is it *alive*?" My question is answered when a patch of mud slides open to reveal a huge, yellow reptilian eye. The slit-like pupil expands and contracts, then swivels to rest on Galatea, who is standing right next to what I'm now realizing is, maybe, a snout.

"Oh, dear," says Sam in a tiny voice.

The mound lets out another thundery growl and heaves itself up out of the water. It has a long, bumpy tail and a snout full of mossy green fangs. Its legs are thick as tree trunks. Its nostrils blow out a breath that smells like rotten meat in the sun.

And I thought the other gator was big.

Somehow, the crane doesn't seem bothered at all. It just shuffles its wings.

Galatea moves to stand before us, sword high. The gator growls at her, baring its fangs—and I see something stuck in them. "Galatea, stop! Don't make it angry!"

"What do *you* suggest?" she says.

"Look at its teeth! The bottom ones! Doesn't that look like a crown piece?"

She sucks in a breath but doesn't have time to reply before the gator opens its mouth and roars. A wave of hot, stinking breath washes over us with enough force to blow our hair back, the stench so awful I can taste it thick and oily on my tongue. Then it lunges. We scatter out of the way just in time to avoid the swipe of its massive snout, which flings mud in all directions and sends big waves rolling out to splash against the tree trunks.

"Stay back!" Galatea shouts at us. "I told you—I'll handle any overgrown lizards!"

But I can't stop looking at the white crane. It's just perched there, totally calm, even as the gator lets out another roar and swings its head angrily. The crane bends its graceful neck, poking its beak into the mud on the gator's back—and the gator freezes in place. Its growl cuts off abruptly. The crane digs around for a couple of seconds, then stops to gulp down a fat, wriggling beetle. As soon as the crane lifts its head, the gator starts growling again.

"Did you guys see that?"

"See what?" says Galatea.

"The crane did something to calm it down. Don't attack—just look." The crane bends down to continue rooting around in the mud, and again the gator stops growling and goes still, looking for all the world like a dog enjoying a round of ear skritches. "See? Calm. And the crane's not scared at all."

"Juniper," says Galatea, "that bird's brain is the size of an olive."

"I trust the bird's instincts over yours, no offense," I tell her.

"Yes offense! Obviously that's a yes offense!"

"Just let me try something," I say.

As the crane digs for bugs and the gator's eyes slide shut in contentment, I wade over to its huge, bumpy tail. Then, bracing myself for the yellow eyes to snap open in fury, I stand on my tiptoes and reach up to scratch the gator's back. One moment passes. Two. The gator doesn't whip around to bite my head off. I freeze when it starts growling again, but it doesn't attack, and I realize there's a different quality to the low, rolling noise. I swear, I think it's purring. Do alligators purr? Surely not. But this one is.

I glance back at the others. Sam and Ollie splash over to help me scratch the gator's sides, but Galatea just stands there, sword forgotten in her hand, staring at me with an odd, unreadable expression.

"Now would be the time to move," I say, and she blinks as if coming awake.

"Right. Yes," she says, coughing a little. She wades over to the gator's snout, where its curling jowls reveal the crown piece stuck between two fangs. "Er, keep—scratching."

"You got it, Princess."

Not that I've ever scratched a gator's back before, but this one is definitely more muddy, less scaly than a normal gator's. Sam, Ollie, and I are clawing at a layer of cool, wet mud. At one point, my fingers dig deep enough that I can feel something firm and smooth under the mud, some sort of flesh. A body in a shell.

Galatea waits for the gator to let out a long, gusty breath, then pokes at the crown piece with her sword. It doesn't move. The gator's purring stutters but goes on. She tries again, and this time the piece shifts but still doesn't dislodge, and one of the gator's brilliant yellow eyes slides open.

It looks directly at me, its pupil a black furrow in a field of grain. The now-familiar voice of Dreamtender rips through my mind.

BEWARE THE TALES THAT HEROES TELL
THE ONE WHO LIES IS NOT WHO FELL

Galatea gives the crown piece a last hard poke. It tumbles out of the gator's mouth, and she dives to catch it before it hits the water. The purring cuts off. Yellow eyes fix on Galatea, and the gator lets out a furious roar, a noise that shakes the trees and causes tremors in the water. She leaps out of range of its snapping jaws, and Sam, Ollie, and I do the same to avoid a swipe of its tail. However, the gator is already starting to shrink. Mud slakes off it, revealing wet, bumpy skin. Same as the magic forest in the Old Barn, the dream ends in moments. The gator shrinks smaller and smaller—the crane finally hops off its back, landing on a nearby branch—until there's nothing but a small green frog treading water in front of us. It blinks twice, then swims away.

"Well," says Galatea, shoving the wet hair out of her eyes. "*Well.* I suppose that's that."

"Good job, team," Ollie says faintly.

I wash the mud off my hands, then dig the other crown piece out of my backpack. Galatea takes it, biting her lip, and fits the two fragments together. They fuse magically with a pulse of cold yellow light, forming what looks like about half of the Crown of Horn. There's still a big chunk missing. Galatea's face falls.

"Hey, it's okay," I tell her. "It looks like Sam's theory was spot-on. I bet we'll find the last piece at the junkyard."

And then you can go home, I don't add.

"That's right," says Sam, swishing her glasses in the water and wiping them clean on her shirt. "Now all we've got to do is find our way back to the road. Luckily, I've got my compass."

Ollie thunks his forehead against her shoulder. "Thankful for you every day, dude."

17

It takes forty minutes to get back to the road. On the way, the four of us try to keep our mouths shut for fear of accidentally swallowing a mosquito, but it's hard not to talk about the things we've seen over the past two days. Galatea, for her part, feels confident that none of the animals involved have been oneiroi, except for the creatures that attacked us outside the barn. Rather, she's certain that each piece of the broken crown acts like a seed wherever it falls. Its magic sinks into the earth like roots, transforming its surroundings. The first piece of the crown touched a puddle and turned it into an enchanted pool. The second probably got nibbled on by a curious frog and turned the frog into its wildest dream—that glorious creature of the swamp.

Galatea frowns when I tell her about hearing Dream-tender again. *"Beware the tales that heroes tell,"* she repeats. *"The one who lies is not who fell.* What does that mean?"

"No idea," I say. "I wish she'd be a bit clearer."

"Indeed, I do as well. That mosquito is absolutely feasting on your arm, by the way."

I crush the mosquito and wipe the blood on a cypress trunk.

Back on our bikes, we head east out of town. The pavement falls away under our tires, one long, winding gray stretch in the muggy afternoon sun. Green presses in on either side, long grass and scrub trees, pine and palm. The air is thick with singing. All those katydids and hidden frogs. (I will say, I'm glad we didn't move somewhere cold and wintry. I've never seen heavy snowfall in real life, but it makes me nervous, the way it hides an entire landscape, turning the tangled growth and colors to a flat, blank white, as if erasing them. A field gone one color. How weird is that? Although I guess it could be fun to make snowballs and stuff.)

We're pedaling and pedaling, and sweat's trickling down my face, and I'm thinking we should stop for a water break, when a building finally swims out of the heat waves ahead. We turn into a gravel parking lot outside a trailer-sized office. The sign says: CYPRESS AUTO SALVAGE. WE TRADE CASH $$$ FOR SCRAPS. Behind the trailer, a chain-link fence blocks off a field of scrap piles and junk cars.

"I can feel it," Galatea says, fingers pressed to her forehead. "Maybe...there?" She points at the yard behind the office. I try not to sigh. With our luck, the last piece of the crown will be buried under a heap of rusty metal.

Satisfied with her findings, Galatea marches right over to the gate in the chain-link fence, which is padlocked shut. Her hand goes to her sword.

"Oh my god. Galatea, hold on," I say. "We can't cut our way in; we'll get in so much trouble. They won't care that we're on a quest," I add when she opens her mouth. She closes it again, annoyed. "Let me check if anyone's in."

I peek into the window. There's someone behind the counter, sort of draped over it as if asleep. Huh. I slip inside, squinting in the dimness. The guy behind the counter doesn't stir. He's sprawled loosely with his face smooshed on the countertop, arms dangling at his sides. My heart beats a little faster. That doesn't look like a normal napping position. Is he okay?

The guy lets out a loud, rattling snore.

The other three enter behind me, staring.

"I can't imagine he'll be giving us much trouble," says Galatea.

Ollie goes over and pokes the guy in the shoulder. No reaction. He just lets out another goose honk and keeps snoozing. There's a puddle of drool under his cheek.

"Is it...magic?" I ask. "Or do we think this is just something he does?"

"I'd wager he's affected by the dream," Galatea says. "Don't worry. I'm sure he'll wake up when the dream breaks. Let's get on with the search, shall we?"

"Fine, but we're not cutting our way through the fence."

"No need," says Ollie, straightening up from behind the counter. He jangles a ring of keys in the air. "Something tells me Snorlax won't be missing these anytime soon."

We go back outside, where Ollie tries a few keys before one successfully opens the padlock on the chain-link gate. The junkyard is lined with rows of ancient-looking cars, plus piles of scrap: car tires, farm equipment, household appliances, strips of corrugated metal, random odds and ends. There are a couple of big machines near the back, like the kinds that crush cars into cubes.

"Should we just...each pick a pile and start searching?" I ask. "Shout if you see something that looks like a crown piece?"

"Sounds good to me," says Sam.

So, we get to work.

I'm digging through a pile of scrap metal, trying really hard to not do anything that would require a tetanus shot, when I suddenly hear a snorting noise. It sounds like a big animal, maybe a dog. I glance around. "Guys? Was there a 'beware of dog' sign?"

"I don't think so," Ollie calls from the next aisle over.

"Huh. Never mind."

I catch a glimpse of Galatea in the next aisle over. She's turned away from me, hair shifting like dark water in front of her face.

The problem with Galatea is that I want to look at her all the time. Even when she's not talking or fighting or doing much of anything, really. Even when she's scowling and swatting mosquitoes. When I look at her, I can feel something stirring in the pit of my belly, a small animal waking from hibernation, ears pricked. Or maybe it's a cicada having slept its fill, ready to crawl out into the sunlight and scream. I do kind of feel like screaming. I want to be her friend, but it's different than it is with Sam and Ollie, and I know why, but I wish I didn't. I can't like her. Not like that. She's from another world. She's a princess. She's leaving as soon as possible, and then I'll never see her again. Probably not even in my dreams. Whatever strange magic connected us, I can't imagine it will survive her leaving. The last thing I need right now is a hopelessly doomed...you know. Crush.

Another snort. Okay, that definitely sounds like an animal.

I round the next pile of scrap and come face-to-face with a bull.

Not just any bull. No, this is not your average cow. He's made of scrap metal, his body clearly harvested from the piles of junk. His heaving sides are corrugated metal, his legs made of jointed machine parts, his hooves shiny gray steel. Smoke trickles from his nostrils like car exhaust.

His eyes are white-hot, glowing points. Two long, deadly looking horns curve out of his head. They're both made of twisting metal, but one has a tip that looks an awful lot like a shard of actual animal horn, glinting in the sun like a pale flame.

The bull looks right at me.

THE ONE WHO SPOKE THE TRUTH AT NIGHT

WILL TURN AGAINST YOU IN THE LIGHT

"Gah!" I say, hand flying to my head. Then I freeze. The bull paws at the dirt with his hoof. I've never been quite so vividly aware of how soft and fragile I am. I would be so very, very easy to impale, like a pink marshmallow on a stick.

"Nice bull," I say. "Niiiiice bull."

"Juniper!" Galatea appears behind the bull. Its head whips around with a noise like rusty hinges. "Don't just stand there, you fool! Get out of the way!"

She takes a running start like an Olympic gymnast and leaps into the air. Her sword flashes, her expression a snarl of concentration, her hair streaming behind her like ribbons. Time slows as I watch. Her feet hit the bull's back, and the sword comes swinging down. Metal strikes metal with a starburst of orange sparks. But Galatea's sword doesn't cut the bull. It doesn't even make a dent; it just skates off sideways, sparking. The bull bucks its hind legs, and she's thrown from its back, landing hard on the ground.

"Galatea!" I cry out. The bull's head swings back around to focus on me.

Sam and Ollie run around the corner and skid to a stop when they see the mechanical bull. He's pawing (hoofing?) at the ground again, smoke blowing from his nostrils. He lowers his head in preparation to charge toward me. There's nothing else to do. I turn tail and run as fast as I can. The chain-link fence is thirty feet away, twenty, ten. The bull's hooves are thundering behind me. At the last possible moment, I veer sharply sideways, elbow hitting the chain-link. Then I'm scrambling away, expecting hot breaths on the back of my neck and sharp horns stabbing into my ribs.

But the bull is much bigger than I am. He can't change direction in time. He runs full tilt into the fence, sparks flying where the chain-link buckles and wraps around his body. I race back to my friends. Galatea's on her feet again, eyes wild as they rove my face. "Juniper! Are you hurt?"

"I'm fine," I gasp. "The bull's horn—it's part of the crown!"

Right now the bull's tangled in the fence, but he won't be for long. There's the sound of tearing metal. My friends and I run toward the back of the yard with the big machines and junker cars. We dive behind a car and crouch there, hidden from view. My chest feels like someone took a jar of angry hornets and shook it hard. There's another awful rending noise, and I hear the bull moving around, rusty joints squeaking. Ollie drops down to peer out from under the car. "It's coming this way!" he says.

Sam's fingernails dig into my arm. "What do we do?"

For once, Galatea looks as helpless as I feel. Then Ollie says, "Wait! I have an idea!" Before any of us can react, he's making a mad dash for one of the machines—one with a huge, circular yellow magnet dangling off the crane arm. He clambers up the ladder, the ring of keys he stole from behind the counter jangling in his hand.

"Do you know how to work that thing?" Sam shouts.

"No! Of course I don't! But one of these controls has to be for the magnet!" The machine roars to life. He yells over the rumbling engine, "Guys! Lure it this way!"

"Oh my god," says Sam.

"The mag-what?" says Galatea.

"Lure it," I mutter. "*Lure* it? Lure it how?" But I think I already know the answer. That bull is just dying to charge us like we're matadors.

"Will someone *tell me what a magnet is*," says Galatea.

I point at it. "Big yellow swingy thing!"

"*What?*"

"NOW!" Ollie yells, and a loud, bone-jittering hum fills the air.

"Oh my *god*," Sam says again. I grab Galatea's wrist, yanking her up after me, and all three of us jump out from behind the car. The bull spots us at once. It's huffing and puffing, dragging a whole section of torn-up chain-link fence behind it. White-hot eyes zero in on us, and it lowers its mighty shoulders, preparing to charge.

I stop dead. "Galatea, wait! Stay back! The magnet's super powerful! It'll get your sword!"

"What?"

"Stay back! Just trust me!"

She's beginning to look seriously ticked off. I wish I had time to explain the concept of magnets, but I do not. Scowling, Galatea moves back a few steps, watching intently. The bull lets out a bellow and charges. Sam and I dart under the giant magnet. I can feel the magnetic pull on the button of my shorts, the only metal I'm wearing. We're gripping each other's hands, sweaty palms slipping. I can hear Sam's hard, shallow breathing. The bull's pounding toward us—its course is set, it won't be able to change direction—twenty feet left between us, then ten—

We spring apart, leaping sideways out of the bull's path. *CLANG*. With an enormous crash, the entire bull flies up and connects with the bottom of the magnet. It howls in fury, legs kicking at the air.

Galatea jumps into action. She climbs halfway up the ladder and leaps onto the top of the giant swinging magnet. She left her sword on the ground, but she doesn't seem to need it. The bull's head is within reach. She leans over the side of the magnet, one leg hooked around the thick chain attached to the crane arm, and grabs at the bull's horn, the one tipped in bone. Red-faced with effort, she pulls with all her might—and with a *CRACK*, the horn comes free. The bull's enraged roar is abruptly silenced. It stops thrashing and goes still, hanging from the magnet like any other collection of spare parts.

Ollie cuts the power to the magnet. All the bits of metal that made up the bull clatter to the ground, lifeless. He turns off the engine, and everything is suddenly so quiet in the wake of all that roaring and bellowing. He clambers out of the machine while Galatea hops down and retrieves her sword.

"I cannot believe that worked," says Ollie.

"Good thinking on your part," I say shakily.

"Thanks, thanks. It's what I do."

I look at Galatea. "I got another bit of prophecy from the bull. It said, 'The one who spoke the truth at night will turn against you in the light.' "

She frowns. "Well, that certainly sounds like it's about Dreamtender. *Spoke the truth at night*—god of dreams. *Turn against you in the light*—betrayal. Attacking the island, or...something. Whatever it is. A bit simple, really. She's just telling us what we already know."

"Why would she warn us about her own evil plans?" I ask. "I still don't get it."

"Who knows? More importantly..." She holds up the crown piece, beaming with triumph. "The third piece! The final one! Finally! Sam, you're brilliant."

Sam gives a modest shrug and adjusts her glasses. "Yeah, I know."

It's the moment of truth. We take out the other part of the crown. Excitedly, Galatea fits the new piece into the old. They fuse together with a pulse of light.

But something's wrong.

The crown isn't whole.

There's still a piece missing. A big shard of bone.

Galatea looks at the still-broken crown like it's a small, dying animal, something tragic and grief making, devastating. "No," she says. "No, that's not—it was supposed to be—that was the last one! Sam's theory! This was supposed to be the last one!" She turns the crown over in her hands like she's hoping to find another piece stuck to it somewhere. "The school is the focal point. Barn, swamp, junkyard. How could it not...?"

"We'll find it," I tell her desperately. "We will. The eclipse isn't until tomorrow night, yeah? We have time. We have all of tomorrow to figure out a new plan. Okay?"

"Maybe we can retrace our steps," Sam offers.

"Yeah," I say. "We'll find it. No matter what."

Galatea just nods, silent. Sam, Ollie, and I exchange

worried looks. Then Sam checks her phone. "We should get out of here before the guy behind the counter wakes up," she says. "Plus, it's almost dinnertime. My parents will be expecting me home. Meet up again in the morning?"

"Sounds good," I say, trying to sound more hopeful than I feel.

18

Half an hour later, I'm pushing open the door of Elmo's Diner. "Now, I don't know what princesses eat," I say. "But trust me, any place with all-day breakfast is heaven. This is gonna blow your mind."

Galatea makes a noise. "Juniper, I really don't—"

I can tell from the pause that she's gotten her first whiff. I can't help it—I grin.

"Gods-all." She inhales deeply through her nose, eyes wide. "What's...What am I...What is that smell?"

"That," I say grandly, "is Diner Smell."

The dinner rush at Elmo's is no joke. Mom and Dad and I have only been here a few times, but it's never not busy.

There are four families ahead of us when I give my name to the host, so we take a seat in the waiting area in the warm, buttery sunlight. Galatea hasn't stopped looking around with a mix of fascination and wariness, eyes lingering on the other families. The hostess calls a name, and a pair of dads gets up, wrangling their shriek-laughing toddler. Galatea keeps taking deep breaths, nostrils flaring. I can't even imagine what it would be like to experience my first Diner Smell at the ripe old age of twelve. I think my brain would implode like a dying star.

"It's coffee," I tell her. "And pancakes. Waffles. Hash browns. Buttered toast. Bacon and sausage. Fried chicken. Fried blueberry muffins. Maple syrup." The fried blueberry muffins are a house specialty at Elmo's and are just bonkers good. They're not deep-fried, just cut in half and pan-fried with butter and sugar. If magic exists in this world, it would be in those muffins and the making of them.

"Let's see, what else.... Oh, eggs, obviously. Fried, scrambled, sunny-side up.... Biscuits and gravy. Coffee cake. French toast."

"Are we attending a banquet?" Galatea looks down at her borrowed T-shirt and mud-flecked jean shorts in dismay. (My parents think we're having dinner at Sam's, so we couldn't go home to change. Oh the tangled webs we weave.) "You had me wear *this* to a *banquet*?"

"Not a banquet, just a diner. This isn't a fancy place. You look fine."

"Oh, thanks ever so much."

Before long, the hostess calls "Harvey" and leads us to a table. Part of why I like this place is that it feels so familiar. Diners are the same pretty much everywhere, you know? There are the mini pitchers of maple and blueberry syrup, bottles of ketchup and Tabasco, the sticky tabletops and laminated menus, the roar of conversation and clinking silverware, and the occasional clang from the direction of the kitchen. Galatea picks up the menu in front of her and immediately looks overwhelmed.

"Can you read it?" I think to ask, not sure how the language magic works—that glowing spell she did on her throat.

She nods. "I can read it. But I don't know what any of these words mean. What on earth is a waffle?"

"Don't worry, you're about to find out. I'll do the ordering."

The waitress appears and gives us a skeptical look. "You gals got any grown-ups with you? Who's paying?"

186

"I have money from my mom," I tell her, which is a lie. The truth is I'm dipping into my stores of collected Christmas-cash-from-relatives-who-don't-know-me for this. (Usually, I spend this money on art supplies.) I brought a thick envelope of it along with me today. Part of me was hoping we could do something fun like this, though I wish it could've been a meal of victory, not defeat.

"All right, all right. What can I get started for you?"

I order a combo that comes with pancakes, hash browns, bacon, sausage, and eggs, plus a side of waffles, two orange juices, and two fried blueberry muffins. The full experience. The waitress takes our menus and bustles off to the next table.

"Where's the music coming from?" Galatea asks, twisting around in her chair. "I don't see any musicians."

"Oh. Okay, so, there are no musicians playing it right now." I try to figure out how to explain the concept of recorded music. Suddenly, I can't remember anything I ever learned about sound waves or whatever in school. "Um...In our world, when someone is playing music, we can record them using, um, technology, like a special machine. And then we can play the music later...on a different machine." I point to one of the speakers on the ceiling, currently crackling out some old-timey, jazzy sort of song. "It's coming from that thing."

"Are those machines common? Do you have one?"

"Yeah. I mean, sort of. You can play music on lots of, um, lots of devices. I'll show you on my phone later."

I slide my phone across the table. It's my dad's old iPhone, the screen all scratched up from living in his pocket alongside his keys. I hit the button to make it light up, and there's my lock screen—a photo I took in the Texas desert, red dirt and blue sky.

"It looks like a window," she says. "What is this place?"

"The desert outside the city where I grew up. My dad used to do scientist stuff out there sometimes, like taking soil samples, so I'd go along with him. It's my favorite place in the world."

"I always wanted to go traveling with Father," Galatea says quietly. "But by the time I was born, his traveling days were over. He had a kingdom to serve."

I can't imagine having a dad like Galatea's—a *royal* dad. My dad is a dork who loves Lord of the Rings and historical fun facts and crossword puzzles and wearing socks with sandals and the desert. I try to picture him wearing a shiny crown, shouting orders or writing decrees or whatever it is that kings do. The idea makes me want to laugh. Dad would totally hate that. He doesn't even like bossing me around. He'd be the chillest king ever, but I don't know if kings are allowed to be chill.

"But your dad's on a voyage now, right?"

She bites her lip. "Yes. He left to find answers, to find some way to help the island. He thought perhaps my mother could help. However, my father and mother only met the one time, when Father traveled to the Arkhean empire before I was born. He met my mother there, on the shores of the Sea of Koraxa—a salt-sea, so different from the Cloud Sea. Have you seen one? You must have them in this world, yes?"

I nod. "We have lots of seas—salt-seas, I mean. And oceans. I've never been to one, but I've seen them in pictures and movies and stuff."

"Oh." She looks a bit disappointed on my behalf. "I've only been to Arkhea once, when I was very small. Father took me, and I saw the salt-sea up close for the first time. Before that, I'd only seen it from the sky. There are days when the Cloud Sea parts and you can stand at the edge of the island and see all the way down to the water and the Arkhean coast. Father must have hoped that my mother, with her ability to wield divine flame, could help him save the island—or that she could ask her own father, the ocean god Seabreaker, for help. He first went to Arkhea to search for her on the shore, but she wasn't there. The other nymphs said she'd gone east, out to sea. Father came home briefly and made preparations to go on a longer voyage. He told me he'd be gone no more than half a year, even if he couldn't find Mother. He said—he *promised* he'd return." She's fiddling with a napkin, folding it into progressively smaller squares. "That was... That was six years ago."

Six years.

"Galatea, I'm so sorry," I say helplessly. Based on what she told me, I assumed her dad had been gone for a couple of months. But six *years*.

"He's alive," she says. "I know he is. I'd—I'd know if he wasn't; I'm sure of it. He will return someday and tell me stories of all his adventures. My father's a hero, you know. He's very brave and clever. He wouldn't..."

I wait for her to find her voice again, and she quickly does.

"This isn't the first time the island has been in grave

danger. Years ago, just before I was born, our island was cursed with an unnatural drought. Crops withered, animals starved, and the people were terrified. That time, my father saved the kingdom. He prayed to Skyrender, who saw the bravery in his heart and agreed to help him. Skyrender told my father where to find the source of the curse. It was a witch—she was hiding in the mountains—and he went there to confront her. The witch challenged Father to a battle of wits, and he won. By her own terms, she was forced to break the curse and leave the island forever. Rain fell again that very same day. Our people were saved. They loved Father. Everyone did. Even Skyrender did—that's when he gave my father the Crown of Horn and the sword I carry now as rewards for his heroism. Father treasured the crown and sword above all other things, keeping them safe in the secret compartment in his rooms. I'm sure he's been doing countless heroic things on his voyage, helping anyone who crosses his path—people who need him much more than I do—and that's why...that's why..."

"Hope you gals brought your appetites!" The waitress reappears and starts laying out plates of piping-hot food: fluffy pancakes with paper cups of whipped butter; crispy, salty-smelling hash browns and bacon; and fried eggs with

soft, oozing yolks. The golden-brown fried blueberry muffins. Orange juice in those tall plastic cups textured like
frosted windowpanes.

"Not a banquet, my foot," says Galatea.

The food's arrival seems to have distracted her from
thinking about her dad, the broken-open expression
wiped off her face, but I'm still on it. *I'm sure he's helping
people who need him much more than I do.* How could
that be true? Who could possibly need him more than
his own daughter, his own kingdom? The Isle of Kypros
is literally going up in smoke, and Galatea's been dealing
with it *alone*? Ruling the island alone, for six years? She's
twelve years old! We're not supposed to be in charge of
people's lives! It's not that I don't think she's capable of
being a good ruler. I'm sure she's good at everything she
does (except singing). And clearly she's willing to do anything to save her kingdom. But she shouldn't have to. She
shouldn't have to carry this burden alone. I mean, where's
Skyrender in all this mess? Where's the king of gods? He
helped Galatea's father get rid of that witch, so why isn't he
helping Galatea now?

"Juniper. *Juniper.*" Galatea snaps her fingers an inch
from my nose.

I twitch back to reality. "Wh—oh. Sorry. Um. Let's eat?"

"Please. I'm starving. Though…I admit I'm not sure where to begin."

"Here." I spread the soft whipped butter over a pancake and drizzle it with a generous amount of syrup. "Try these first. Then the bacon."

We don't talk for a few minutes, too focused on eating. I pay attention to what Galatea likes best: She prefers pancakes to waffles, sausage to bacon. She loves the hash browns, especially with a bit of Tabasco, and—to my deep satisfaction—devours her fried blueberry muffin in about three seconds flat, princess manners forgotten. The only thing she doesn't seem to like is the orange juice.

As we finally start to slow, a question occurs to me. I've been replaying her words in my head, everything she said about her dad.

"Galatea," I say, and she looks up. Her gaze is just as intense in a bright, sunny diner as it is in my dreams. "If your parents only met once, in Arkhea, how did you end up on the Isle of Kypros?"

"Mother sent me on a sea dragon. Are you going to finish that?" She's eyeing the remaining half of my blueberry muffin.

I push the plate over. "Go for it. Your mom did *what* now?"

"She fastened me to the back of a sea dragon and bade it deliver me to my father. I don't remember it, of course; I was a newborn. I don't remember anything about Mother. She sent a letter along with me, tucked into my blankets. Father showed me as soon as I was old enough."

"What did it say?"

"It said, *Her name is Galatea. Please be good to her.*"

I wait, but she doesn't continue. "That's all it said?"

She takes a huge bite of muffin and chews for a long time. "What else is there to say?"

A thousand things, I want to shout, but I hold my tongue. I'm aware of the tense set of Galatea's shoulders, the way she's hunching into herself a little, in a way that feels so unlike her—I'm the one who curls inward, not her. Not Galatea with her straight spine and fierce eyes, her tendency to charge first and think later. I only met her a couple of days ago, but I know it's wrong to see her so...defeated.

I have to get her home. I'm going to.

Instead of prying deeper into her past, I take a swig of orange juice. "So, you don't remember the sea dragon. But you've seen other dragons, right?"

"Oh," says Galatea, and I know I'm not imagining the relief in her voice. "Oh, well, of course. The mountains are crawling with them."

I lean forward over the table, nearly putting my elbow in a puddle of egg yolk. *"Please tell me about the dragons."*

She smiles, and tells me.

19

That night, I return from the bathroom to find Galatea flipping through my sketchbook. (My parents said yes to a second sleepover so fast it almost broke the sound barrier. I just know they're hoping Galatea will be my new best friend.) My face goes hot. "Uh! Hi! Hello. What are you doing?"

"I'm just looking."

I fight the urge to go over and snatch the sketchbook out of her hand. She's already seen some of it, but there's a lot of *other* stuff she hasn't seen, and some of that stuff is embarrassing. "Um...looking at what?"

"A lot of insects, apparently. You've got quite the obsession."

"Okay. And, um, why are you looking?"

She raises an eyebrow at me. "It's a book of your artwork. I'm curious."

For some reason, that makes my face go even hotter. "Okay. Well. Can I just—if you're gonna look, I'd rather show you myself. Just…promise you won't laugh."

"What? Why would I laugh?"

"Just promise you won't."

"Do you really think that poorly of me?" she asks quietly.

I blink. "Huh?"

"Never mind. Yes, Juniper, I promise not to mock your life's work."

That's a bit of a stretch, but whatever. We sit on the floor with our backs against the bed. I want to sit crosslegged, but that would mean putting my knee on her leg, so I do not. I flip past the pages she's already seen, past the fully inked and colored dream scenes to the pages populated by messier, unfinished sketches. I point out a sketch of Poppy the honeybee.

"Um, this is the main character of the story I'm working on. It's a comic, which means it's a story told with illustrations instead of just words. Poppy is a honeybee. And this is the other main character, Shriek. She's a cicada." I turn the page. "Uh, more bugs. This is mostly gonna be bugs. Just warning you in advance."

Galatea leans closer, examining the sketches of worms, beetles, moths, spiders, and so on. "They're incredibly detailed."

"Yeah. I use a lot of references, like pictures and stuff, so I can learn how to draw them."

"You put a lot of work into this."

"Oh. Yeah, I guess. I really like art."

"So I've gathered."

I flip through a few more pages of Poppy and Shriek, then a few pages of background practice: sketches of flowers and knotted tree roots and mushrooms, Poppy's hive with its honeycomb halls. I begin to relax.

I turn the page. Four Galateas glare up at me with graphite eyes.

The real Galatea makes a small noise of—surprise? I can't tell. I've drawn her in four different poses, all of them suited for battle. One with her sword raised, one with it swinging in a low arc, one with her holding a shield I've never actually seen her with—I made it up based on illustrations of ancient Greek armor. The last pose is the most embarrassing one. I drew her with blood on her chin, dribbling out of her mouth, fists up and knuckles scraped. I cough a little. "Um. I thought—um. Remember how I thought you were a figment of my imagination."

"Hmm." She reaches out to touch the last drawing, the one with the blood. "Is there a reason I look like I've gone ten rounds with an angry lion?"

I cough again. "No reason in particular. I just, you know, in my head, I thought it might be cool if you were some kind of warrior...."

"A warrior." There's an odd note in her voice. "I suppose you're right." For some reason she sounds almost disappointed.

"No," I say. "I don't think that anymore. Don't get me wrong, you're the only kid I've ever met who knows how to sword fight, but that's not—um, that's obviously not the only thing you are. If that makes sense."

"What else am I?"

"A princess, for starters."

"Mm."

"Is there something else you want to be?" It feels bold to ask.

"No." A pause. "It's silly."

"That's not the same thing as no."

"Yes, well. For a princess it is."

"Hey." I poke her on the kneecap. She looks up to frown at me, and now we're looking at each other—sitting thigh to thigh and looking at each other, the sketchbook forgotten on my lap. This close, I can see the silver scales in her gray eyes, fish darting in wintry waters. Her features are wide and strong and crooked. Her nose is so good. "Galatea," I say. "What's your silly little dream?"

"I..."

"I'll tell you mine if you tell me yours."

"I know yours," she says, gaze flicking to the sketchbook. "It's this."

Something leaps in my belly. Another fish flashing its scales in the light, body wriggling madly in the air. *Yeah, this.* Sure. Sure. "So, it's your turn."

"I...I want to be a physician," she says in a rush. "A healer. I have a natural affinity for it through my sea nymph blood, but that's not why I like it. I just *do*."

"Hang on. Is that how you helped save that guy who got his arm bitten off by a dragon?"

She smiles before continuing.

"Ever since I was small, I've been fascinated by the palace physicians. I used to sneak down to the physicians' clinic all the time, hide in the cupboards, and watch them work. A few years ago, right after Father left, the head physician caught me spying. I was certain she'd scold me for abandoning my lessons, but instead...instead she tied my hair back and fetched a stool for me to stand on and put me to work crushing herbs. After that I stopped hiding." Her eyes are bright as stars. "As I grew older, she let me see more. I watched her cut a man's chest open to remove a painful growth on his lung. I watched her amputate infected limbs—lose the leg to save the life. I watched her deliver babies and ease birthing pains."

Holy crow. She's watched actual amputations. And babies being born. Oof. "Oh my god, wait." I'm connecting the dots. "Is that why you were so good at using the scalpel during art class? And chopping vegetables for dinner? And why you weren't shocked by Noah's nasty skin flakes?"

She glances at me. "You notice a lot."

"Ha ha," I say. "Just an artist thing."

"Hmm."

Then her pleased expression clouds over. "Of course, my fantasy couldn't last forever. Father left; things got worse and worse with the island.... My duty is to my people, my kingdom, above all else. I don't have time for silly dreams."

"They're not actually silly," I tell her. "Like, I know you have a responsibility to your people, but...dude. You're twelve. You're a kid. You shouldn't have to save the kingdom all by yourself." I wish I was better with words. I wish I knew how to make her understand what I'm trying to say. "It's not wrong to want something different. You're not doing anything wrong, okay? I mean, so far, you've done everything right. You've done everything you could."

"I haven't done anything right," she whispers. "I snuck into Father's rooms and touched the crown—I gave Dreamtender unfettered access to my head. I stole the crown and Father's old sword for this—this failed quest. I tried to get to the Isle of Dreams, but I couldn't even do that right."

"It's not your fault the crown malfunctioned." I try to

ignore the flutter of guilt in my belly. I still haven't told her about the wish. I mean, I still don't know if there's anything *to* tell. "None of this is your fault. It just stinks."

"It . . . stinks?"

"Oh, sorry. Um. If something stinks, that just means it's a crappy situation. It's not fair; it's unfortunate. It's not your fault, maybe it's not anyone's fault, but you're the one stuck dealing with it. And that stinks. It stinks like rotten eggs."

"I see," she says, seemingly taking that in.

"Galatea. It's cool that you want to be a doctor. That's like really cool. I wish you could."

"I wish that, too," she says carefully, as if testing the words for the first time.

I can't bear the quiet. My skin feels electric. I turn to the next page in my sketchbook, unable to look at her. "Uh, anyway, here's . . . Oh. More drawings of you. Sorry." At least the ones on this page aren't too humiliating. She's not bloody-knuckled, for one. I just sketched her in a couple of basic standing poses to practice the folds of her clothing.

"Don't apologize. You're somewhat talented, you know."

"Thanks," I say flatly.

To my surprise, she laughs. "No, I'm sorry. You're very talented, Juniper. You always get my nose right."

And suddenly I'm trying not to blush.

We go through the rest of my sketchbook, talking in soft voices. But finally, we're both yawning. We can't put off bedtime any longer.

Lying there in the dark, as I realize it might be our last night together, my chest aches in good and terrible ways. It's the same swelling, rib-expanding feeling I used to get after a good rain. It rained so rarely back in Texas, it was a thrill every time. Something as ordinary as crossing a parking lot was transformed, made new and exciting by the sleek, shiny pavement; the puddles swirling with gasoline color; all the dust washed out of the air, each cool breath hitting the bottom of my lungs like a coin in a wishing well.

I imagine reaching out in the dark, my hand drifting like a rowboat between us. I don't know what I want. For her to laugh again. For her eyes to land on me and linger. I want to do something heroic in front of her. I want to rush into a burning building to save kittens. I want a super-villain to attack during gym class and have it look like all hope is lost, until I reveal that actually I have elemental superpowers and I can make tree roots erupt through the floor of the basketball court to wrap around the villain and, like, thwart him. I want Galatea to watch the whole thing, in awe of me. And I want to be a version of me who doesn't notice or care if girls like Galatea are in awe of her at all.

"Hey," I whisper. "Can I show you something?"

She doesn't answer for so long, I think she's fallen asleep. Then she says, "Yes."

"Here." I grab my phone and a pair of earbuds off the nightstand. I pull up my music app and dangle one earbud over the bed for her to take.

"What is this?"

"It's called an earbud. You put it into your ear."

"For what purpose, exactly?"

"You'll see."

I don't know what kind of music she's used to. Dragon pipes, I guess. What else? I think she mentioned the lyre? And singing for sure. Everyone everywhere sings. I flick through a couple of playlists until I find one of my favorites. I turn down the volume and wait until she's fitted the earbud into her ear—I can see half of her frown in the moonlight, her elbow moving as she fiddles with it. I hit PLAY.

She jerks, startled, and opens her mouth to tell me off. Then she goes still.

"Oh," she says.

Warm guitar plucks behind a low, pretty voice. I'm listening through the other earbud. The song is about wishing you were the moon. I think of Galatea like that: a landscape faintly illuminated. Even with one ear uncovered, I feel very abruptly cut off from the world. It's just me and Galatea and the earbuds, the wires trailing between us. We are two telephone poles on a lonely highway. Two glow-in-the-dark stars on a bedroom ceiling.

The last chords fade out into a breath of silence before the next song starts. I peek at Galatea over the edge of the bed. Her eyes are closed—I can't see the glint of them. She's lying on her back. I was never aware of Riley like this. With Riley, it was like we were the same creature, braided together. We used to play in her backyard, pretending to be wolves. We straight up howled at the moon, and I'm sure the whole street heard us. I felt so formed around her that I think if we really had turned to wolves, we would have been a single loping animal that would have run out to the desert and howled.

But with Galatea, it's like I'm a sensory instrument

tuned to her every movement. Like I'm picking up earthquakes, my needle leaping over the paper, measuring tremors.

We need to find the final missing piece of the Crown of Horn so she can leave.

So she can go home, to save her home.

It's okay. It's okay.

I close my eyes. It takes a few more songs, but in the end, I do drift off to sleep.

20

In my dream, there's Galatea, a twig of flame against the smoke-dark sea. Her hair streams in the wind. She's standing in the surf, the tide flooding in around her shins, soaking the hem of her chiton. It's nighttime. Three moons shine brightly in the sky.

"Galatea," I say.

She walks out of the water toward me. Then she takes off running down the beach.

"Hey—wait!"

I chase after her. The beach is surrounded by rocky cliffs. Up ahead, two huge gates are set into the cliffside. They're like thirty feet tall, shaped like arches, and look to be made of pale, intricately carved stone. These must be the Gates of Horn and Ivory—which means this must be the Isle of Dreams. I realize I've seen it before. We've been here before. *Juniper, the tide's coming in.*

As I chase Galatea down the beach, the scenery changes. The beach becomes a forest, the sound of waves turning to the rustling of branches in the night breeze. The sand turns to fallen leaves underfoot. Trees press in on all sides.

It's the forest from the Old Barn.

"Galatea, wait up!"

I burst into a clearing, and there she is. She's standing in the middle, in the moonlight. She turns to look at me. A shadow passes over the moons, throwing the forest into darkness. Galatea starts turning to ivory. It happens so quickly, as always. It's only moments before she's a frozen statue, staring blankly in my direction with white, unseeing eyes. It's worse now that I know her in real life. Now that I've seen her perpetual frown, the way her brow crinkles in thought.

A crack appears in the statue's chest, over the heart. The crack spreads, branching out like veins, until the statue looks like a broken eggshell. It crumbles into a pile of dust.

WHERE ONCE WAS LIFE, NOW ONLY DEATH

AT DARKEST HOUR, FINAL BREATH

"Hey!" I call out. "Dreamtender!"

The forest rings with silence.

I cup both hands around my mouth. "Dreamtender! I know you can hear me! I know you're here somewhere!"

Silence.

"What do you want from me?" I shout. "Why are you telling me these things? Why can't you just stop speaking in riddles and tell me what you want? I just want to save the Isle of Kypros!"

Something steps out of the trees. It's a deer—a doe with a coat the light brown of mushroom gills. She picks her way over the crunchy leaves without making a sound and stops a few feet away. Her big, soft eyes bore into mine.

BRING ME THE CROWN

HELP ME SAVE HER

"What—*what*?" I breathe, but the doe's already bounding away into the shadows. "Wait! Come back!"

My heart's racing. That didn't sound like the other prophecies. That sounded like a cry for help. Like Dreamtender wants to save someone—save *her*. Does she mean Kypris? Galatea? She must mean Kypris, right? After all, she's been the one showing us the dreams of Kypris getting stabbed.

What if the hooded figure isn't Dreamtender?

The events in the dreams—what if she's trying to *stop* them from happening?

Bring me the crown. Help me save her.

"I want to," I tell the forest. "I want to help. But the crown is broken. It has a piece missing. It won't work."

Silence. I feel a twang in my chest, like a string being plucked. I remember sitting in my bedroom that night, putting the finishing touches on a portrait of Galatea. Gazing into her gray eyes. Feeling that pull. Making that wish.

I raise a hand and trace a shape into the air. A thread of yellow light flows from my index finger. I draw the outline of the Crown of Horn: a twisting circle. The light casts a gentle glow on the forest floor.

"I wish you were here," I say.

An object drops into my hand. Then the forest swirls like melting wax, colors dripping down the sky to reveal a black dome, no moons or even stars. Clutching the final piece of the crown in my hand, I let the dream world swallow me and spit me out, awake.

21

It's not yet dawn. I lie still for a moment, sipping at the air.

The piece is still in my hand. I did it; I found it. We can fix the Crown of Horn now. We can make it whole. And she can leave.

She will leave.

My heart hurts. I think if I concentrated, I'd be able to hear it cracking right down the middle, crumbling into bloodred ash. I've barely known her for two days, so why does it hurt so bad? It's worse than moving more than a thousand miles, worse than saying goodbye to home and Riley, worse than realizing Riley didn't miss me like I missed her. Why is this so much worse? I just want a little more time to know her. Galatea, razor-sharp and glorious in a fight. Galatea, loudmouth lower-your-horns-and-charge princess. Galatea, warm and true.

I do not get to keep her. I'd be terribly selfish to try, so selfish I can't even consider it. Not when her home hangs in the balance.

So, I scoot to the edge of the bed. She's awake, face turned toward me, though she wouldn't have been able to see me from the floor.

"Hi," I whisper.

"Hi," she whispers back.

And I hold up the crown piece. Galatea's eyes go round.

"Juniper," she breathes. "How?"

"I found it in a dream. Well—I sort of drew it? But, Galatea, something else happened in the dream. Something you should know. I talked to Dreamtender."

"You *what*?"

"First, she told me another prophecy: 'Where once was life, now only death. At darkest hour, final breath.' It sounds like another reference to the Triple Eclipse? But I asked her to please say something else, and she said, 'Bring me the crown. Help me save her.'" I look at Galatea, expecting to find her as stunned as I feel. Her expression remains flat. "Galatea. Dreamtender's trying to tell us something, but I—I don't think she's threatening Kypris and the island, like we thought. I think there's something else going on. It sounded like she's trying to *help* Kypris."

"Help her with what?" Galatea asks.

"I mean, I don't know. The thing we keep seeing. The attack. We've never actually seen the hooded figure's face, you know? Maybe it's not Dreamtender. Maybe she's trying to stop whoever it is from going through with it."

"The thing you keep seeing."

"What?"

"The thing *you* keep seeing," she repeats. "You are the one who witnesses the attack. I have never seen it. I only see you."

"Okay...? What does that have to do with anything? I'm telling you, I think we've got it wrong. I think the hooded figure is someone else."

"But who would it be?" she snaps. "If it's not Dreamtender, who is it? There's no other suspect, Juniper! No one else has any reason to harm Kypris!"

"But what reason does Dreamtender have? Correct me if I'm wrong, but I didn't think she had any connection to your island at all. So why would she randomly decide to stab Kypris with the freaking legendary Godkiller sword?"

"I don't know! I don't pretend to understand the wicked machinations of her mind, Juniper! She's been exiled for thousands of years. Perhaps she simply went mad."

"But that doesn't make sense. You just said it—she's exiled. She's *been* exiled. By the king of gods, right? Skyrender? The big one? Why would she come out of exile after thousands of years just to attack Skyrender for no reason? And then, after he defeated her and sent her back into exile, why would she break it *again* to attack a random island goddess? No offense, but it's not like Kypris is the queen of gods. She's not super powerful or, like, important to Skyrender. Right? So why on earth would Dreamtender attack her? And then why would she say, 'Help me save her'?"

"I...I..." Galatea looks furious. "I don't know. It doesn't matter!"

"Of course it matters!"

"It doesn't, because Dreamtender is clearly lying to you. Where did you learn this? In a dream? That's her domain, Juniper. And of course she wants the crown back. She always has. It's an object of power. It will allow her to leave the Isle of Dreams. Remember the Oracle's prophecy? *To rightful owner must return the stolen crown, or all will burn.* Tell me, what does that sound like to you? Because to me, it sounds like a threat. It sounds like Dreamtender wants her crown back so she can leave her island and go to mine. To attack Kypris. When I go to the Isle of Dreams, it won't be to return her crown—to do exactly what she wants. I'm going to stop her from hurting Kypris if it is the last thing I do. And if that means destroying the Crown of Horn in front of her so neither of us can leave, *so be it.*"

"But…" I struggle for words. "But…I just…I think there's something we're not seeing. Some part of the picture. I mean—I mean, why is the island disappearing in the first place? Where's Kypris now? Where's she been?"

"I. Don't. Know. If I knew, I would have fixed it already."

"Listen. Let's just think for a second, okay? Let's—let's stop focusing on the details and look at the big picture. Your dad got the Crown of Horn from Skyrender, right? As a reward for completing a quest?"

She nods warily.

"What was the quest?"

"You know this. I told you."

"Just tell me again."

"There was a witch in the mountains," she says. "She cursed the island with unnatural drought. My father prayed to Skyrender for help. Skyrender came to his aid and told Father where to find the witch. So Father went and found her and defeated her in a battle of wits, and she was forced to break the curse and leave forever."

"And then, as a reward, Skyrender gave your dad the Crown of Horn."

"Yes. And my sword. As I *said*."

"But why? What does the Crown of Horn have to do with a witch?"

"Oh, for—it doesn't matter, Juniper! It was a token of Skyrender's appreciation!"

"That's some token," I say. "Dreamtender's incredibly powerful magic crown. And your dad had to hide it? Keep it a secret from everyone but you? Is that normal?"

Her lips thin. "Can you please get to the point?"

"The point is, I don't know the point. The more I think about it, the less it makes sense. Maybe there's something more to the story about your dad."

The moment I say it, I know I've made a mistake.

Galatea's expression slams shut. "My father is a hero,"

she snarls. "He saved our kingdom. And someday when he returns home, his people will rejoice. As will his daughter." The last word comes out shaky. "You don't know anything. You have never stepped foot on my island. You've never been to my world. You don't know the names of our gods, nor their stories. You don't know my people, my family, my blood. You don't know me."

I want to. I've been trying. I don't have the guts to say it.

"You're a fool to trust Dreamtender. Don't you see? This is what she does, Juniper! This is why she was exiled. She lies. She sends nightmares and false prophecies. Somehow, I didn't think you'd fall for it."

"You know what I think?"

"Oh, I'm sure you'll tell me."

"I—I think you're not listening to me because you're too scared to admit you're wrong."

"Scared?" She scrambles to her feet, crossing her arms over her chest. There's a storm in her face, in the dark slashes of her brows. "Scared! Oh, please. You're one to talk."

"What?" I say. "Wh—of what, the monsters we keep running into? Okay, yeah! Sure! Sorry I froze up when there was a giant metal murder cow trying to trample us to death! In my world we don't generally get those!"

"I'm not talking about the monsters," she says. "I'm talking about everything else. You said you've been *lonely*. Well, whose fault is that? I went to your school with you. I watched you all day. You didn't talk to anyone unless they spoke to you first. You didn't even look at anyone. If you're lonely, it's because you're scared to try."

I'm shocked silent.

"You're a—a coward." She's clearly trying to sound ruthless, vicious, but her voice is coming out shaky. "You're a coward, and you're trying to turn me into one. But I don't have that kind of time. I must save my kingdom. Give me the crown piece."

I hold on to it. "You're making a mistake."

"The mistake," she says, "was coming here in the first place."

It's an echo of what she said when she first got here, and now it stings so much more. Hot tears spring to my eyes. There's a horrible fuzzy pressure in my nose. Great. Just great. I try not to blink. The absolute last thing I need is to start crying in front of her. "Fine," I say. "Fine, then. Here."

I hold out the crown piece. She takes it wordlessly. We're avoiding each other's eyes, staring resolutely in different directions. I'm trying so hard not to cry. Galatea gets the rest of the crown from under her pillow, hair falling to hide her face. She fits the pieces together, there's a breath of light, and the Crown of Horn is fixed. It's whole. The pale bone gleams in the first tinge of dawn. It is beautiful, I think dully. A crown fit for a god. For a princess.

Galatea gathers her things: sword in its sheath, sword belt, clothes. She changes out of her borrowed pajamas right there. I stare at the floor, face burning. The silence is thick and heavy. She puts on her sandals.

I can't believe this is it.

Will we ever see each other again?

The words stick in my throat with the unshed tears. How humiliating would it be to say something like that, when she just made it crystal clear she thinks I'm a coward and she wishes we'd never met? I didn't realize it until right now, but I guess I thought maybe she liked me a little— like as a *friend*—and clearly I was so, so wrong. I've been wrong this whole time. Oh, god.

Then Galatea's done. There's nothing left to do. She's standing there in the middle of my bedroom, just the same as when she arrived, except this time she's holding a crown. And also, everything's different. I awkwardly get out of bed, figuring I should at least stand up to say goodbye.

"Well—I'll be going," she says.

I manage to nod.

"Thank you," she says stiffly, "for your help."

I nod again.

Galatea takes a deep, steadying breath, as if preparing to plunge underwater. She lifts the Crown of Horn onto her head. It starts glowing the moment it touches her hair. Her lips move, mouthing, *Isle of Dreams. Isle of Dreams. Isle of Dreams.*

The glow spreads to her body. So many times I've seen her swallowed, only this time, it's light that eats her instead of bone. She's so bright. A little sun in my bedroom, flinging off clementine rays like she's making her own dawn. Light must be shining out the window, illuminating the side yard, gilding the morning dew. It burns to look at her, but I can't look away. Her shape imprints itself on the insides of my eyelids, black negatives of her popping up in the corners of my vision. I'm looking and looking and looking and looking, *looking, Galatea*—

And she's gone.

It's soundless. No boom or lightning crack or fizzle. The light fades, leaving my room seemingly darker than before, and I'm alone. She's not here. She'll never be here, not ever again. I could search for her in every corner of Cypress and Florida and the entire world beyond and I'd never be able to find her. She is gone from this world, and she's not coming back.

The tears brim over. I sink to the floor, bury my face in my knees, and cry.

I sit there until the tears turn to sniffles and a throbbing headache. It's almost six when I finally lift my head. Good thing I don't have school today. I just want to curl up in bed.

Miserable, I get to my feet. My sketchbook's sitting on the desk. I know it's a terrible idea that will just make me more sad, but I can't help but pick it up and flip through the pages. All those drawings of Galatea and her world. Galatea in a battle stance, Galatea glaring defiantly, Galatea giving a small, crescent-moon smile. Galatea, Galatea, Galatea. I can't believe I *showed* her these.

I turn the page to a colored-pencil drawing of the temple. At least this one doesn't have her in it. There's just Kypris and the hooded figure. My fingers brush over the pencil lines. Will I never learn what the dreams meant and why I had them? Will I truly never learn why the Isle of Kypros started disappearing—or if Galatea will be able to save it? What if she can't? What if something goes wrong? What if she gets hurt? I'm helpless.

A breeze ruffles my hair. I blink a little, thinking I should close the window in case it rains. But the window is already shut.

I look back at my sketchbook. Another breeze swirls lightly around me, sweet with the scent of flowers. And the drawing begins to *move*. The hooded figure's cloak rustles in the wind. Same with Kypris's hair. Suddenly, I can smell hot metal and smoke, the same as in my dreams. Stunned, I lean in closer. I watch the hooded figure reach into their cloak, pulling out the giant sword. I watch them strike. I watch Kypris fall. Then something happens that I've never seen before in any of the dreams. Because this time, I don't turn to look at Galatea. This time, I see everything. The hooded figure pulls the sword back out of Kypris's chest as she falls—then they let go of it, and the sword falls to the ground at their feet. And it changes. It transforms from the giant golden sword, Godkiller, into a small, plain bronze one.

I know that sword. Even when it's a small sketch that's barely an inch long.

That's Galatea's sword.

I remember what she said about Godkiller: *One of the few weapons capable of spilling divine blood—of taking an immortal life. The stories claim it was created so mortals could defend themselves against the gods.*

So *mortals* could defend themselves.

I look up from my sketchbook. "Oh, crap."

22

I don't expect Sam and Ollie to reply to my texts at six AM on a Sunday, but they prove me wrong immediately.

Me

we found the last crown piece.

galatea left.

but i realized something and now i

think she's in serious danger

i'm going after her

Ollie

hhello??????

elaborate???????

Sam

1. Please explain

2. Go after her how?

Me

i think i know of a way. long story

not sure it'll work

but i have to try

Sam

We're coming with you.

Me

what??

nooo no no no

its ok

i just wanted to tell someone

I put my phone down and start ripping blank pages out of my sketchbook. Over the next ten minutes, I tape them to my bedroom wall in the shape of a big, tall arch. I go to grab a pencil—and nearly jump out of my skin when there's a loud tap on the window. I whirl around. Sam and

Ollie are standing outside. Ollie gives me a friendly wave and mouths, *Open up!*

Gaping, I go over to open the window. "What are you guys *doing* here?"

"Did you seriously think we'd let you jet off on a grand adventure all by your lonesome?" Ollie says, hoisting himself up onto the sill. "Please. All for one and one for all, dude. Here, move back." He drops to the floor and offers a hand to help Sam through.

"Good morning," she says. "What's the plan?"

"Um..." I wasn't expecting to have to explain it. Suddenly, this feels like a confession. "Okay. Um. You know how Galatea didn't mean to end up here? And she thought it happened because the Crown of Horn like malfunctioned or something?" They nod. "Yeah. So, here's the thing. That night, before she appeared, I drew this picture of her. I mean, at the time I didn't know it was *her*; I thought I was just having dreams about this girl." Ollie waggles his eyebrows. I want to die a little. "And, well, I sort of made a wish. And a couple hours later, boom. Galatea."

"What kind of wish?" says Sam. "What was the exact wording?"

"Oh my god. Um, it was 'I wish you were here.'"

"Ohhhh," she says.

Ollie gives me a grin that makes my face burn hotter than ever.

"Yeah, so, I have no idea what's going on, but I think I'm connected to this somehow. To the dreams, the magic. I don't know how it works, but—I have to try. That's how I found the last crown piece—in my dream last night, I drew it and then wished it into existence. So, I'm going to try this wishing thing again. But this time, I'm not going to draw her. I don't want to bring her back here and risk the crown breaking all over again, not when we're so close to the Triple Eclipse. Galatea went to the Isle of Dreams, so that's where I'm going."

"Where *we're* going," says Ollie. "Also, how?"

"Besides the crown, the only way to enter or leave the island is through the Gates of Horn and Ivory. So...I'm going to draw the Gate of Horn." I hesitate. "But *seriously*, you guys don't have to come. I don't know if this will work. And if it does work, best-case scenario, we're going to an island with an angry god and her freaky shape-shifting bird minions. It's going to be dangerous."

"Super dangerous." Sam's eyes glint behind her glasses.

I'm beginning to think she is a little bit nuts. Like a mad scientist. That's cool.

"Sounds like it," says Ollie. "Sam, just out of curiosity, what happens if this taking-a-portal-to-another-dimension thing goes wrong?"

"There's no way to know for sure," she says. "But theoretically? Physicists call it *spaghettification*, and it's exactly what it sounds like."

He turns faintly green but doesn't back down.

There's no time to worry about spaghettification. I grab a pencil, go to the wall, and start drawing. My hand moves quickly over the taped-up pages. I'm picturing the Gate of Horn from last night's dream, where I found Galatea on the beach. A huge, pale arch set into the cliffside. It's okay if the details aren't perfect. I know what I'm drawing. I hope that's enough.

I feel a thread in my heart, tugging. I remember this feeling. It's the same one I felt in the art room on the night of the dance, and after, when I couldn't sleep before finishing her portrait. I don't know what it is, but there's something pulling me toward her. Something that connects us, that spans the space and time between us, no matter how far away we are. I just feel her. Wherever she is, I can find her there.

"June."

I don't remember closing my eyes. I open them and gasp. My drawing, which stretches across all the pages, has begun to glow. The lines burn gold, forming the outline of a gate large enough to walk through, right there on my bedroom wall. The air shimmers around it, though it's not giving off heat. This is cold fire, the greenish gold of divine flame. The middle isn't blank wall anymore. It's a black void.

The Gate of Horn burns before us.

Sam blows out a breath. "That's a portal," she says. "That is a portal."

"I can't believe it worked," I say.

"Let's hope it continues working," Ollie says nervously.

We look at one another. "You're sure?" I ask. They nod, faces cast in the cool light. "Okay. Maybe we should..."

I hold out my hands. They each take one. Together, we step through the gate.

The world falls into a blackness like the space between stars. I can't see anything, not even my own self. It's like

I'm a pair of disembodied eyes floating in an endless void—except I can still feel Sam's and Ollie's hands in mine. It's super weird. Then there's a squeezing sensation, like I'm being crushed in a giant fist. It knocks the breath out of my lungs, and it's all I can do to not let go of my friends' hands. I can't breathe. Trying not to panic, I concentrate on that *feeling* in my chest. The tugging thread. I imagine it unspooling before me, leading the way. I can follow it out of the dark.

And I do.

The squeezing stops. Light floods my vision as my senses return all at once. I suck in a breath, then another, and hear Sam and Ollie doing the same thing on either side of me. We drop one another's hands, examining our surroundings. We've arrived on a cold, misty beach. Dark sand stretches out to meet the steely-gray ocean. Waves crash against the shore, and behind us the sea cliffs rise up to a pale, wintry sky. Hundreds of black-winged birds are perched along the top of the cliffs, staring down at us. Oneiroi. They definitely know we're here, but they don't seem primed to attack. They're just watching, silent. I try not to shiver.

"Kinda wishing I'd brought my bat," Ollie mutters.

Then there are the massive gates set into the cliff face, framing huge, dark caverns. We're standing right at the mouth of the Gate of Horn.

My portal *worked*. I'd be proud if I weren't so worried about everything else.

"First things first," I say. "We have to find Galatea."

As if on cue, all the oneiroi take off at once. They flock into the sky and move as one, flying off down the beach.

"If I had to guess," says Ollie, "I'd say we should go thataway."

We chase the black-winged oneiroi down the beach, shoes slapping the sand. The wind whips at my face, tugging at my hair with icy fingers. The flock of oneiroi dips behind a jutting cliff up ahead, and we have to splash into the water and wade out in the shallows to get around it. When we round the cliff face, I see two figures standing a ways up the shore. One is Galatea. The other must be Dreamtender.

They don't seem to have noticed us. I motion at Sam and Ollie to move back into the shadows of the cliff. Meanwhile, the oneiroi settle like black snow on the rocks behind Dreamtender, hundreds of pairs of beady eyes all fixing on Galatea.

"What are we waiting for?" Ollie whispers.

"I don't know," I whisper back. "I just want to make sure...." Even as I say it, I realize I really *don't* know. We're too far away to hear anything. And if the roles were reversed and Galatea were here to save me, she wouldn't hide in the shadows and wait for the right moment, which might never come. She would just charge.

I look at my friends. They meet my eyes readily, solemn and square-shouldered. They've got my back, and I've got theirs. Galatea needs us. There's nothing to wait for.

"Let's go," I say.

Turns out charging through knee-deep water is *not* as cool as, like, charging onto a battlefield. Ideally our grand entrance would have involved a lot less sloshing and slogging and nearly falling over. By the time we reach the shore, both Galatea and Dreamtender are very much aware of our arrival. Galatea's back is turned to us—she seems unwilling to take her eyes off the god—but Dreamtender is watching us approach with something almost like amusement. We splash out of the surf and onto the sand, and at long last I see Dreamtender up close—not as a statue in a temple, but in the flesh. The god of dreams has to be at least seven feet tall and is wearing a silvery gown that cascades to the sand at her feet. Her black gaze pierces mine, pinning me in place. I get the distinct impression that she can see right into my head, into my heart.

SO YOU BROUGHT MORTALS.

Her voice rolls over us like thunder. I'm braced for it, because I've heard it bouncing around my skull before, but Sam and Ollie both cringe.

"I did not bring them," Galatea says without turning around. She's got her sword raised in front of her, blade pointed at the god, bronze oddly dull in the misty, overcast light. "Juniper. Sam. Ollie. What are you *doing* here?"

"Galatea, you have to listen to me," I say urgently. "Something's wrong. Dreamtender's not the villain here."

"We *had this conversation*," she snaps. "Don't be a fool, Juniper! Leave this place! Go home! You're not a part of this—it's between me and her!"

Dreamtender's eyes flash. I DON'T KNOW, HALF-LING. PERHAPS YOU SHOULD LISTEN TO THE MORTAL.

"Shut up!" Galatea says. "You can't trick me! I won't fall for it! It's been you all along, threatening my home, my kingdom, my people! *When third eye closes, she is lost. The Isle of Kypros pays the cost. Flame to ash and flesh to*

234

bone, what was reaped must now be sown. I'm not stupid, Goddess! I understand the prophecy! I know you're planning to hurt Kypris while her divine powers are weakened by the Triple Eclipse, to make the Isle of Kypros disappear forever—all to get revenge on a god who has nothing to do with us!"

"Galatea, you're *wrong*!" I shout.

She shoots me a blazing look. "Shut up, Juniper!"

"No! I—I won't shut up! You're wrong, and I can prove it." I stride forward, putting myself between Galatea and Dreamtender, with my back to the god. Galatea's staring at me like I've gone bananas, and maybe I have, but I know I'm right about this. "Galatea. Give me your sword."

"*What?*"

"I can prove it. Just give me your sword."

Her grip tightens on the hilt.

"Galatea," I say, quieter. "I'm with you. Please trust me."

Her eyes, the same gray as the sea, dart to the god standing silently behind me. For all I know, Dreamtender's raising a hand to smite me into a pile of dust. But I don't turn around to check. I keep my eyes on Galatea. I look and look. Just a couple of hours ago, I thought I'd never see her face again.

Slowly, she lowers the sword and holds it out for me to take. The moment I wrap my fingers around the hilt and she lets go, the sword transforms from plain bronze to a shining, fiery gold metal, like a tongue of flame forged into the shape of a weapon. The blade doubles in length and width. The giant sword looks like it should weigh a hundred pounds, but in my hand it's light as a feather.

"This is the sword from the dream," I say. "This is the sword that hurts Kypris."

Where Sam and Ollie look a bit confused, Galatea's face is a rictus of shock.

"You said it yourself: The legendary sword Godkiller was created so mortals could defend themselves against the gods. But what you didn't know—what I didn't realize until I saw it in a sort of...*vision*, after you left—is that the sword *only works* for mortals. It only reveals its true form if a mortal is wielding it. If a god or anyone else with divine blood tries to use it, it'll just act like a normal sword."

"But..." Galatea gives a slight shake of her head. "But that's..."

"The hooded figure can't be Dreamtender," I say. "It has to be a mortal. And—and I'm so sorry, but I think I know who it is. I mean—who it *was*."

"...Was?" she says.

I nod. "All of it already happened. It happened twelve years ago. Our shared dream wasn't a vision of the future. It was a memory of the past. Right, *Goddess*?"

CLEVER MORTAL, she says silkily. CAREFUL WHERE YOU POINT THAT THING.

"But that doesn't make sense!" Galatea insists. "My sword can't be—it can't have been, this whole time—Juniper, that's the sword I took from Father's room!"

"Yes." It feels awful. "Yes. I know."

"But..." Horrified realization dawns, even as she keeps shaking her head in denial.

"Galatea." I step closer. "Please. I think we should hear Dreamtender out. Whatever she's got to say, I think we should listen."

Her throat moves as she swallows. Another beat of hesitation. Finally, she whispers, "All right. All right, Juniper. I'll...I'll listen."

We look at Dreamtender. "Tell us the truth," I say. "Please."

ALWAYS, says the god. Then she snaps her fingers.

23

Thunder booms overhead, rain pours down in sheets, and the sky cracks with lightning. The four of us are standing in a huge, smoking crater, like the crash site of a meteorite. Galatea, still white-faced with anger, shoves the wet curls out of her eyes. "What is this? Where are we?"

"Look!" Sam says. "Over there."

I squint through the rain to see a pale shape at the very bottom of the crater.

It's a god.

Dreamtender is lying in a motionless heap on the scorched earth. Rain drums down on her, mingling with a pool of golden blood. Suddenly, this place seems familiar, and I realize I've seen something like this before, but from a different perspective: the dream where I saw someone fall out of the sky during a storm, getting struck by lightning on the way down. I remember Galatea wondering if the falling figure was Kypris. Could it have been Dreamtender instead?

Are we in a memory?

Just then the rain stops. The storm fades in a matter of moments, almost in time-lapse, the clouds parting to let down streams of sunlight. Dreamtender remains unmoving, her face hidden by a tangle of bloodied hair.

There's a noise from above. I look up to see someone stick their head over the lip of the crater. Their face is shaded by a straw hat, like they're a farmer.

They call down, "Hey!"

Sam and Ollie look to me. "Um. Hi?" I call back with a tentative wave, not sure if this is real or not, a dream or not, a memory. The person doesn't seem to hear me. They jump down into the crater, landing lightly as a cat despite the thirty-foot drop, and walk over to Dreamtender. Wherever their feet touch the earth, green grass and wildflowers bloom and die. This is the woman with the magic feet. This is—

"*Kypris*," Galatea cries out. "Kypris!"

I catch her wrist, letting go just as quickly. "She can't hear you."

"What?"

"She can't hear you. We're in a memory. Look."

Kypris, goddess of Kypros, sinks into a crouch beside Dreamtender's prone form. She hasn't so much as glanced in our direction, giving zero indication that she can see or hear us.

"Goddess!" Galatea tries again, to no response. She falls silent, watching as Kypris appears to examine Dreamtender's wounds—of which there are many, judging by the amount of blood. It looks like she lost a fight with a lawn mower. And she still hasn't moved a muscle. Who or what could have injured a god this badly?

Then Kypris does something that shocks me: She reaches out and pokes Dreamtender in the shoulder. Just... pokes her, like a kid with a bug.

"Hey," she says. "You all right?"

There's a long pause.

I'VE BEEN BETTER, says the god of dreams.

"I can see that much," says Kypris. She's not using a godly voice like Dreamtender does; she sounds normal, mortal. "You're bleeding from about a hundred different places. Got in a fight with the lord of the sky, did you?"

HE STARTED IT.

"Hmm. Well, fear not. This island is my domain. Even Skyrender cannot step foot here unless I allow it. Come to my house, Goddess. I'll tend to your wounds."

Dreamtender finally lifts her head to give Kypris a flat, disbelieving look. Golden blood drips off the end of her chin.

IF YOU HELP ME, YOU DEFY HIM.

"You mean like you did? I heard about that, you know. The Old God who refused to join the New Pantheon, way back when. I hear you got permanently banished to your island, far away from this place. But that was a thousand generations ago. I've no idea why you'd break the terms of your exile to come defy the king of gods all over again, but I'm sure there's a fascinating explanation. I think I'd quite like to hear it."

Dreamtender stares at her—and the scene changes. Now the four of us are in a small, firelit room, shadows flickering on the stone walls. The two gods sit on the stone hearth, Kypris with a washrag and basin of water. A doe is curled up at her feet, big dark eyes fixed watchfully on

Dreamtender. Kypris wrings gold-tinged water into the basin and wets the rag again, dabbing gently at a nasty cut on Dreamtender's arm. I'm all too aware of Galatea standing beside me, close enough that I can feel warmth coming off her skin; I can hear her breaths.

"Why did you defy him?" Kypris asks. "Way back when?"

Dreamtender turns her face to the wall. She doesn't answer.

Then it's daytime, and we're outside in a garden. There's a cow lying on the ground with her head cradled in Kypris's lap, huffing and puffing as she strains to give birth to a calf. Dreamtender is watching them from the doorway of the little stone house. Her eyes swallow the sunlight instead of reflecting it, like black holes. The cow bellows in pain and kicks feebly.

"It's all right," Kypris murmurs, stroking the cow's sweat-soaked neck. "You're all right; you're almost there."

The cow's next bellow curdles into an awful whimper. Her sides heave. Then Dreamtender comes into the garden to kneel beside Kypris and places a hand on the cow's forehead. The cow calms at once, hard animal breaths evening out into something peaceful, like she's having a

242

good dream. I wonder what cows dream about. Mead-
ows, maybe. Clear skies. The moon reflected in the eyes
of other cows, bright coins in the dark. With a final clench
and push, the cow bears her calf. Kypris smiles at Dreamtender, warm and open, brown eyes sparkling like a sunlit
river—

And we're in a beautiful, flowering orchard, petals
swirling in the breeze. I can hear the sound of bells. Then
Galatea says, "Singing cherries." I turn to see her gazing
up at the tree branches, the awed expression on her face
so similar to when she saw the singing cherry in the Old
Barn. She looks close to tears.

The two gods are walking a sunlit path, a basket of
cherries swinging from Kypris's arm. Her mouth is stained
red. "You've enjoyed my hospitality for months now," she's
saying, "yet you refuse to answer a simple question, no
matter how many times I ask. It's really not fair, Goddess.
You're lucky I'm so nice and accommodating. Anyone else
would've thrown you to the Fates the first time you tried to
cook a meal for them. How does a *god* burn a soup?"

Dreamtender rolls her eyes. It's so human it startles me
a little.

Kypris stops to pick another handful of cherries. Both

goddesses are slightly larger than life, standing about seven feet tall, and she can reach some of the highest branches.

"Goddess," Kypris says. "Why did you defy him? Why, when Skyrender and Seabreaker stormed the heavens, overthrowing the Old Gods who had reigned since the dawn of the Kosmos, when it was obvious that any god who refused to join them would suffer the consequences, why did you refuse? Why did you challenge him, when you knew he would win?"

I DIDN'T.

Kypris stills, hand outstretched to the cherries. It's clear she wasn't actually expecting a response.

I WOULD HAVE REFUSED, says Dreamtender. BUT SKYRENDER DID NOT GIVE ME THE CHANCE. MY FATE WAS SEALED THE MOMENT HE TOOK THE THRONE. BANISHING ME WAS HIS FIRST ACT AS KING OF GODS.

"But why?" asks Kypris.

I REMIND HIM OF THE ONLY THING HE FEARS.

"What's that?"

HUMANS.

She frowns. "Why would he fear humans? Skyrender

loves humans. He loves anything that can worship him," she adds darkly.

HE DOESN'T LOVE HUMANS. HE NEEDS THEM. HE NEEDS THEM TO BUILD HIS TEMPLES, TO CARVE HIS STATUES, TO SING HIS PRAISES. HE NEEDS THEIR SACRIFICES. HE NEEDS THEIR STORIES, THEIR SACRED FIRES. THEIR PRAYERS. THEIR BELIEF. YOU AND I BOTH KNOW THAT A GOD WILL DIE WITH-OUT THE BELIEF OF MORTALS. WITHOUT THAT, HE IS NOTHING. HE IS SMOKE AND ASH, A GUTTERED CANDLE. AND I...I AM THE GOD OF DREAMS. BUT TO DREAM IS HUMAN. GODS DO NOT DREAM, NOT REALLY. WE MAY SEE GLIMPSES OF PAST, PRESENT, AND FUTURE, PROPHECIES AND OMENS, BUT WE DO NOT DREAM AS HUMANS DO. NOT ENDLESSLY. NOT ARDENTLY. NOT WITH EVERY CRUMB OF OUR BEING.

Dreamtender tilts her head back, sun sliding over her face.

YEARS AGO, A DYING ORACLE DELIVERED HER FINAL PROPHECY: THAT THE CHILD BORN TO SKYRENDER'S MOST DEVOTED BELIEVER

WOULD SOMEDAY GROW TO DESTROY HIM. AFTER LEARNING OF THIS, SKYRENDER PAID VISITS TO THE LARGEST, RICHEST TEMPLES IN ALL OF ARKHEA, UNTIL HE FOUND A PRIESTESS WHO HAD RECENTLY GIVEN BIRTH. HE TOLD HER TO PROVE HER DEVOTION BY SACRIFICING THE NEWBORN CHILD. SHE DID.

"You're lying," Galatea chokes out, though the gods can't hear her. She's bloodless and trembling; her hands are balled into fists at her sides.

Meanwhile, Kypris is saying, "That's why you broke your exile. That's why you challenged him, after so long."

I WAS NAIVE. I THOUGHT...I THOUGHT PERHAPS I COULD REASON WITH HIM. I WAS WRONG.

"She's *lying*," Galatea says desperately, and the scene changes. We're in the garden, but the plants are all dried up and dead. The air is sweltering, the sun beating down relentlessly. I remember this heat from my dream, the one where I watched Kypris lead a procession of sickly looking animals up the mountain. Now she's standing in the garden, squinting up at the white sun. "Half a year without rain," she says, worried. "Half a year..."

Our surroundings change in dizzying flashes. Plants

wither in the boiling heat—green hills and valleys going yellow, orchards of singing cherries with stark, empty branches. We see a river choked with fish floating belly up, herds of cattle starved to bones, farmers staring in mute horror at barren fields. Then we're in the garden and the mother cow is there, the one who gave birth, and she's lying on the ground again, but this time her sides are just barely fluttering with her breaths. She looks very ill. Kypris is singing to her, stroking her flank.

Dreamtender appears in the doorway.

I LEAVE AT SUNSET, she says.

Kypris's head jerks up. "What?"

YOUR ISLAND IS DYING. YOUR PEOPLE ARE DYING. HE IS PUNISHING YOU FOR HARBORING ME. THE LORD OF THE SKY WOULD SOONER STARVE A THOUSAND MORTALS THAN ALLOW HIMSELF A SINGLE CUT. AND I HAVE CUT HIM.

"No. Don't act rashly. I—I will go to my father. He won't—"

YOUR FATHER SPENDS HIS NIGHTS DRINKING IN SKYRENDER'S HALL WITH THE REST. THEY ARE BROTHERS IN ARMS. IF YOU THINK HE WILL FLY TO YOUR AID, YOU'RE A FOOL.

Kypris rears back, face twisting in hurt. "As soon as you leave this island, you're at his mercy. The last time you fought him, I found you half-dead in a crater. This time... he's that much angrier, Goddess. He's so angry."

NO LONGER WILL I PLAY THE COWARD.

"He'll destroy you! He'll give you a sentence worse than exile—worse than death!"

THEN THAT IS MY FATE.

She turns and goes back inside, leaving Kypris alone in the garden with the dying cow. A tear streaks down her face.

The scene changes.

It's sunset now. We're standing out in front of the little stone house, and for the first time, Dreamtender and Kypris are nowhere to be seen. Exchanging wary glances with Sam and Ollie, I wait for what I know happens next. A figure appears, cresting the mountain path. They're wearing a blue hooded cloak. I feel cold. Galatea's breath stops in her throat. The figure walks up to the door—in the dreams it was a temple, a grand, beautiful temple, but here it's just her house—and knocks.

It swings open immediately. Kypris's hopeful expression drops when she sees the person on her doorstep isn't

Dreamtender. "Good evening, traveler," she says. "You must be lost."

"Do you live here?" the figure asks in a deep, smooth voice. Beside me, Galatea's hand flies to cover her mouth.

"Yes," Kypris says slowly.

"Then consider this retribution." They draw a sword from within the folds of their cloak. And oh, I know this part. I know what comes next.

She has time to look startled. I never saw that before.

The sword—the huge, magical, burning sword, Godkiller—catches the dying light as the hooded figure drives it into Kypris's heart. She chokes. The figure yanks the sword back out, a horrific noise, and lets go of it, stumbling back. It happens exactly as I saw in my bedroom, when my drawing came to life. The moment their fingers leave the hilt, Godkiller transforms into the smaller, plain bronze sword Galatea's been carrying around for days. The one she got from her father. It clatters to the ground.

Kypris falls in slow motion.

NO.

Suddenly, Dreamtender's there, catching Kypris in her arms and sinking to the ground with her. She holds Kypris half-upright in her lap, one hand coming to frame her face.

Blood trickles from Kypris's mouth in a golden line. Her whole front is awash with it, gleaming slickly.

"No, no, no," Dreamtender says in a mortal voice, hand fluttering from Kypris's face to the wound in her chest and back again, as if afraid to touch. She hasn't even looked at the hooded figure. "Goddess, look at me—you're all right. You're going to be all right."

Kypris seems unable to speak. Her gaze is fixed on Dreamtender's face. Her breaths are wet rasps clawing their way out of her throat. There's so much blood. Molten gold pools beneath her, soaking Dreamtender's clothes. Her lips move faintly, mouthing something, but no sound comes out.

"Kypris." Dreamtender's voice breaks. "You can't die. You're a god; you can't die." Her eyes catch on the discarded sword. Her features go slack with horror. "No. How...?"

The hooded figure falls to their knees. "I—I didn't," they stammer, sounding petrified, "I didn't—didn't know— I didn't know, I, I thought—he told me she was a witch...."

WHO SENT YOU HERE?

Trembling, the figure shakes their head hard. "I, I..."

WHO. SENT YOU. HERE.

"The lord of the sky," they breathe. "But—but I, I didn't—he told me—I thought she was—"

SHUT UP.

She turns back to Kypris, cradling her closer. "It's okay," she whispers, even as tears brim in her black eyes and fall to land on Kypris's cheeks. "It's okay. You're going to be all right, Goddess. I'll make sure of it."

She presses her face to Kypris's hair and takes a deep, shuddering breath, then places her hand over Kypris's heart. Golden blood oozes up through her fingers. The skin beneath her touch glows with the light of divine flame. And I see it: the ivory. It's radiating out from Dreamtender's hand in white tendrils, like veins of ice, spreading across Kypris's body. Ivory creeps over her skin, her clothes, freezing her in place—turning her into a statue. Her face is the last to be swallowed, her fawn eyes fixed on Dreamtender until the very end. Then it's over. Where moments ago there was a goddess, now there is only an ivory statue of a woman half-crumpled on the ground, her frozen face locked in a blank, empty expression.

Wisps of smoke are starting to come off Dreamtender's

body. She pulls her hand away from Kypris's heart to watch her fingertips dissolving into pale, misty smoke. She doesn't look surprised. She holds on to Kypris, not letting go even as the smoke eats away at her hands. Her wrists. Her arms. It's like she used every last drop of her divine power to turn Kypris to ivory, and now she's simply fading away into nothingness. She leans in, resting her forehead against Kypris's, and closes her eyes as the smoke takes her. A few more moments, and she's gone. The Crown of Horn falls through the suddenly empty air, landing on the ground beside the statue.

For a moment, all is still.

The hooded figure lifts their head. On their knees, they shuffle over to pick up the fallen crown. They're weeping, shoulders heaving as they gasp for breath. And finally, they take off their hood to reveal their face.

Galatea lets out a sob.

The figure is a gray-eyed man with dark, silver-shot hair. I've never seen him before, but I would recognize him anywhere. Galatea looks so much like her father.

King Machus clutches the Crown of Horn in both hands. His face is wet with horrified tears. He looks at the statue of Kypris, her body curved in that dying position, held upright by an embrace that no longer exists.

"Goddess," the king says. "I'm so sorry."

The last rays of sunset slip beneath the horizon. Clouds gather in the starry purple sky, and a cool rain begins to fall, speckling the dead grass. The earth drinks, greedy. Raindrops slide down the statue's ivory cheeks. The dream ends.

24

I taste salt. We've returned to the beach on Dreamtender's isle, wind tossing up sea spray. I'm once again holding the magic sword. Dreamtender herself stands before us. She looks exactly the same as she did when we got here—a tall, imposing figure with eyes black as voids—but in my head, she's entirely changed. Now I know her as the god who broke her eternal exile because the king of gods did something horrific to a priestess and her baby. I know her as the god who knelt beside a bawling cow to soothe it with good dreams, who planned to offer herself to Sky-render to save the Isle of Kypros—and its goddess—from his wrath.

You loved her, I think.

Dreamtender's voice echoes in my head alone:

I DOOMED HER.

"It's not true!" Galatea says, choked with tears. "My father wouldn't—he *wouldn't.*" She rounds on Sam, Ollie, and me in turn, giving us desperate looks. "She's able to create false visions! She could be lying!"

But I can't stop thinking about the catch in Dreamtender's mortal voice when she said, *Kypris.* How frantically she palmed Kypris's face, swept a thumb over her blood-freckled cheek. The look in her eyes as she watched Kypris tend to her animals, her orchards, Dreamtender's wounds. I know she's not lying. That look was the absolute truth. I know it the way you know things sometimes, bone-deep as loneliness, right in the living room of the heart.

"Galatea, I'm sorry," I say.

Her expression collapses.

Sam steps forward. "But *why* did he do it?" she asks boldly. "We all saw his face afterward. He looked so shocked."

GOOD QUESTION, says Dreamtender. ALLOW ME TO DEMONSTRATE.

Her arm moves faster than I can track. She grabs

Godkiller right out of my hand, and the sword instantly turns plain bronze again. Before any of us can blink, Dreamtender plunges the sword into my belly.

Galatea screams. Sam gasps. Ollie lets out a strangled yell. I stand there blankly, waiting for the pain to come—but it doesn't. I glance down. Dreamtender pulls the sword out of my belly, and it doesn't hurt at all. In fact, I don't feel a thing. There's no blood on the blade, no wound in my stomach.

"Oh my god," I wheeze. "You could've just said it can't hurt mortals."

I PREFER THE VISUAL.

She tosses the sword in the sand at Galatea's feet. Galatea scrambles to pick it up and brandishes it. "What does this sword have to do with my father?" she demands.

Dreamtender looks at her steadily. ONLY THE GODDESS AND I KNEW WHY THE RAIN HAD STOPPED. YOUR FATHER, KING MACHUS OF KYPROS, PRAYED TO THE LORD OF THE SKY, BEGGING FOR RELIEF FROM THE DROUGHT. I'M SURE HE SAID HE WOULD DO ANYTHING. THE LORD OF THE SKY FED HIM A SERIES OF CAREFULLY CRAFTED TRUTHS...THEN

TOLD HIM WHERE HE COULD FIND THE SWORD GODKILLER. THAT SWORD HAS A LONG AND STORIED LIFE. AT THE TIME, IT WAS IN THE POSSESSION OF A SEA NYMPH.

Galatea's face turns whiter still.

KING MACHUS WENT TO THE SHORES OF KORAXA. HE FOUND THE SEA NYMPH, AND WOULDN'T YOU KNOW IT: THEY FELL IN LOVE. ONE MONTH THEY SPENT TOGETHER. AT THE END, SHE WILLINGLY GIFTED HIM THE SWORD. HE RETURNED TO THE ISLE OF KYPROS AND DID WHAT HE BELIEVED HAD TO BE DONE. AND YES, PRINCESS GALATEA, NINE MONTHS LATER, A SEA DRAGON SHOWED UP WITH A NEWBORN CHILD STRAPPED TO ITS BACK.

"How do you know all this?" Galatea asks.

I WALKED THE PATHWAYS OF HIS DREAMS.

"What did Skyrender tell Galatea's dad?" I ask. "What carefully crafted truths?"

HE TOLD HIM, A STONE HOUSE IN THE MOUNTAINS HIDES A HEAVENLY FUGITIVE, ONE WHO HAS DEFIED THE GODS AND MUST BE PUNISHED.

A MORTAL WOUND FROM GODKILLER SHALL CAST THE DIVINE FLAME FROM HER BODY. WHEN SHE FALLS, SO, TOO, WILL THE RAIN. Her eyes narrow. KING MACHUS THOUGHT HE WAS LOOKING FOR A HUMAN WHO HAD STOLEN DIVINE FLAME. HE THOUGHT THE SWORD WOULD DESTROY THE FLAME BUT SPARE THE THIEF.

"And it was meant to be you," I add. "Right? Skyrender didn't know you'd decided to give yourself up. He thought *you* would answer the door, not Kypris."

YES, she says. THOUGH I'M SURE HE DIDN'T CARE THAT IT WENT WRONG. IN THE END, HE GOT WHAT HE WANTED. I WAS POWERLESS—I WAS SOMETHING LESS SUBSTANTIAL THAN SMOKE. TWELVE YEARS I HAVE SPENT TRAPPED ON THIS ISLAND, TOO WEAK TO LEAVE WITHOUT THE CROWN OF HORN. I HAVE HAD TO RELY ON MY ONEIROI.

The flocks of black-winged oneiroi, who until now have been watching silently from the rocks, start preening and puffing out their chests with pride.

"Wait. Do you mean, when the oneiroi attacked us...

Was that you trying to *communicate*?" I ask. "And is that why you kept beaming rhymes into my head?"

She nods. I COULD SPEAK ONLY THE LANGUAGE OF PROPHECY.

"So, you're saying I had to fight off a bunch of blood-thirsty nightmare sheep for *no reason*?" Ollie says.

YOUR NIGHTMARES, NOT MINE.

"Then, this whole time, you haven't been trying to threaten us," I realize aloud. "You've been trying to warn us." I look at the others. "The prophecies I've been hearing—*When third eye closes, she is lost. The Isle of Kypros pays the cost*. And Galatea, the one you heard from the Oracle—"

She recites dully, "*Heart and kingdom, land and throne, a goddess sleeps entombed in bone. To rightful owner must return the stolen crown, or all will burn*."

All will burn.

The words thud around us like falling rocks. The crown in question is still perched on Galatea's head. She's stopped crying but looks shattered. I want to take her hand, touch her shoulder, offer some sort of comfort, but I don't know if she'd want me to.

"Father said it was a witch," she says, raw. "He told

me—he told *everyone*—there was a witch in the mountains, and...and he outsmarted her and broke her wicked enchantment, and that was why the drought ended."

YOUR FATHER'S GREATEST FEAR WAS THAT, WHEN THE BARDS AND POETS SANG OF KING MACHUS, THEY WOULD IMMORTALIZE HIM AS HE WAS: A FOOL.

"Okay, stop!" I snap. "Now you're just being a jerk."

A WHAT?

"A jerk."

"Juniper, stand down." Galatea lifts her chin to look Dreamtender dead in the eye. "I've heard enough. Just tell me this. Does Kypris live?"

SHE LIVES, BUT ONLY JUST. I SEALED THE LAST SPARK OF HER DIVINITY WITHIN THE IVORY STATUE. I CAN REVIVE HER, BUT IT MUST HAPPEN BEFORE THE ECLIPSE SHADOWS THE THIRD MOON. TIME IS RUNNING OUT, PRINCESS.

"What must we do?"

GIVE ME THE CROWN OF HORN. I WILL GO TO HER.

"You must take us with you," Galatea says. "You can't leave us here."

YOU HAVE MY WORD.

"Will reviving Kypris save the island?"

THE ISLAND WILL BE RESTORED.

"And what of my people? Are they safe?"

That gives Dreamtender pause. Her elegant brow furrows.

YOU DON'T KNOW?

"What? Don't know what?"

WHEN YOU LEFT THE ISLAND…

She snaps her fingers. We're standing in an ancient-looking city square. All around us, dozens of ivory statues are posed for all the world like normal people going about their business: merchants and vendors, customers crowding around market stalls, children playing in the dust. The square is silent, frozen. In the horizon, I can see the edges of the island continuing to fade, to dissolve into smoke.

Dreamtender quickly snaps us to the beach.

THE FATES OF KYPRIS AND THE ISLAND ARE INEXTRICABLY TWINED, she says. IN THESE FINAL HOURS, AS KYPRIS'S LIFE WANES TO NOTHING, SO TOO DOES THE ISLE OF KYPROS AND THE LIFE IT CARRIES. REVIVING KYPRIS WILL REVIVE YOUR PEOPLE. THIS I PROMISE, GALATEA OF KYPROS.

Galatea swallows. "All right," she says. "All right." She slides Godkiller into the sheath at her waist, then reaches up to take off the Crown of Horn. She moves to stand in front of Dreamtender and sinks to her knees on the wet sand, holding the crown aloft. "Please help me, Goddess."

Dreamtender takes the crown. Her expression doesn't waver as she lifts it onto her head. The moment it touches her hair, something changes about her. She seems to glow from within, not quite with light but with fullness, warmth, and color, as if some essential part of her was missing and she's only just now becoming whole. She's somehow brighter, more vivid, than before.

READY, MORTALS?

My friends and I look at one another. Sam nods. Then Ollie, then me. Then Galatea, her thunderhead gaze locking on to mine. "To Kypros," she says.

25

The Isle of Kypros is almost entirely gone.

It's not even an island anymore. It's the fragments of one: huge chunks of earth and rock floating in the sky in a sea of swirling clouds. I can see hilly peaks in the distance—from my vantage point on a chunk of island that used to be a mountaintop—and a faraway chunk with the glimmer of a city, but so much of what lies between has turned to smoke. Some of the fragments have waterfalls pouring off them, parts of the river that used to cut through Kypros like a shining vein.

Night has already fallen, the sky a deep blue, budding with stars. The three moons are casting light over the vanishing kingdom. One moon is fat and yellow, one smaller and silvery white, the last very small and red as a bloodshot eye. The nearest chunk of island is close enough that I can see tree roots dangling out of the earthy foundations as bits of rock crumble away and disappear into the clouds. From where I stand, I can make out what looks to be the ruins of a house a little farther up the mountainside.

We follow Dreamtender up to the grassy crest. What used to be Kypris's home is now a pile of charred rubble grown over with moss, like it burned down years ago. Among the ruins, there's a weathered, mossy statue. Her ivory face is tilted to the stars.

"She's been here all along," Galatea whispers. "I can't believe it."

Dreamtender goes and sinks to her knees in the ruins beside the statue, hand hovering in the air as if afraid to touch. GODDESS, she says, and nothing more.

Sam points at the sky. "The eclipse is starting!"

Sure enough, all three moons have a growing rim of shadow on one side.

"Hurry, Goddess!" Galatea says. "Do it now!"

YES. Dreamtender reaches out to cup the statue's face.

Suddenly, a flash splits the air inches away from us. A tongue of lightning wraps around Dreamtender's wrist like a flaming rope, dragging her backward across the grass. We whirl around and see a man standing below us on the mountainside, arm still raised from hurling the lightning bolt. The man's posture is calm, casual. He has to be ten feet tall, skin gleaming like polished wood. His robes are the exact blue of the night sky.

I WOULDN'T DO THAT IF I WERE YOU, he says.

"Skyrender," Galatea snarls. "How dare you show your face here!"

HOW DARE I?

The king of gods advances up the mountainside slowly, lazily, like a jungle cat stalking its prey. Dreamtender's lying in the grass, the lightning bolt wrapped around her wrist crackling and shooting off yellow sparks.

IT USED TO BE THAT I COULD NOT STEP FOOT ON THIS ISLAND. Skyrender's godly voice is louder than Dreamtender's, booming like thunder. I want to cringe away from it, to clap my hands over my ears, though I know that won't stop his words from reverberating through my head. It's almost painful. IT SEEMS THAT HAS CHANGED.

COULD IT BE THAT SOMETHING HAS HAPPENED TO DEAR KYPRIS? COULD IT BE THAT THE SPARK OF HER DIVINE FLAME IS ONLY MOMENTS FROM BEING EXTINGUISHED FOREVER? He gives us a cold, cruel smile. HOW UNFORTUNATE.

"Why are you doing this?" Galatea shouts. The four of us are huddled around the statue, blocking it with our bodies, and she shoulders her way in front to stand before us. "What grudge do you bear against Kypris, against this island? What did we ever do to you?"

GRUDGE? Skyrender looks amused. YOU VASTLY OVERESTIMATE YOUR OWN IMPORTANCE, HALF-LING. WHY WOULD I CARE ABOUT A FLOATING SPECK WITH A FEW HUNDRED MORTALS CLING-ING TO IT LIKE BARNACLES? YOUR GOD AND YOUR ISLAND ARE NOTHING TO ME.

"Then *why*? Why not let us revive her?"

I HAVE A SCORE TO SETTLE WITH THE GOD OF DREAMS.

AND I WITH YOU, SKYRENDER, Dreamtender says from the ground. She's struggling to push herself upright, curls of smoke coming off her wrist where the lightning bolt is searing her flesh. ONE THAT BEGAN A

THOUSAND GENERATIONS AGO, WHEN FIRST YOU STORMED THE HEAVENS.

His look of amusement deepens. ETERNAL EXILE WASN'T ENOUGH FOR YOU, THEN? PERHAPS YOU'D RATHER BE CHAINED TO A MOUNTAIN, DEVOURED OVER AND OVER BY STARVING WOLVES, YOUR BODY REGENERATING EACH DAY JUST TO FEED THEM AGAIN IN THE NIGHT. PERHAPS YOU'D RATHER BE THROWN INTO A PIT IN THE DARKEST DEPTHS OF THE OCEAN WITH ONLY YOUR FELLOW BOTTOM DWELLERS FOR COMPANY. OR PERHAPS YOU'D RATHER LIVE THE REST OF YOUR END-LESS LIFE WITH THE KNOWLEDGE THAT IT WAS YOU WHO BROUGHT DEATH AND DESTRUCTION TO HER DOOR. BUT…I SUPPOSE THAT WOULD BE YOUR FATE NO MATTER WHAT. AND I RATHER LIKE THE WOLF IDEA. His expression hardens, all traces of mockery gone. OR, PERHAPS, I WILL SIMPLY FINISH WHAT THAT USELESS WRETCH OF A KING STARTED TWELVE YEARS AGO.

"My father didn't start anything!" Galatea shouts furi-ously. "He didn't want to hurt any gods! He didn't want to kill anyone! You lied to him!"

I TOLD NO LIES.

"You tricked him!"

I GAVE HIM INFORMATION. HOW HE USED IT WAS HIS OWN CHOICE.

"What choice did he have?" She's trembling with rage. "His people were dying! He was desperate to save them! He prayed to you for help, and you deceived him! You used him as a tool of vengeance against Dreamtender!"

YOUR ACCUSATIONS BORE ME, HALFLING.

He snaps his fingers. Cuffs of lightning wrap around Galatea's wrists, forcing her hands behind her back and making her cry out in pain. She falls to her knees in the grass.

"Galatea!" I drop down beside her, steadying her by the shoulders. The lightning sparks and fizzles, giving off a terrible heat. I can smell Galatea's skin beginning to burn. Her jaw clenches as she holds back tears of agony. "Let her go!" I shout at Skyrender.

He doesn't even look at me. He hasn't acknowledged Sam, Ollie, and me, as if regular old mortals aren't even prey in his eyes, just insects to be crushed underfoot.

NOW, GODDESS. He advances on Dreamtender. WHY DON'T YOU GIVE ME THE CROWN?

She stares, thrown. WHAT...WHAT USE IS IT TO YOU?

I THINK I'D LIKE TO VISIT YOUR ISLAND, he says. IN FACT, I THINK I'D LIKE TO VISIT THE INSIDES OF THE MORTALS' HEADS EVERY NIGHT IN THEIR DREAMS. I MIGHT EVEN LIKE TO SHAPE THOSE DREAMS. YOU SEE, GODDESS, SOMETIMES HUMANS DREAM A LITTLE TOO FANCIFULLY FOR MY LIKING. SOMETIMES THEY GET CERTAIN IDEAS—ABOUT THE GODS, ABOUT THEMSELVES—THAT I WOULD PREFER TO DISSUADE BEFORE THEY COME TO FRUITION.

NO, Dreamtender says.

Skyrender lowers into a crouch a few paces away from where she's lying in the grass, so he can meet her at eye level. I'M AFRAID THAT'S NOT AN OPTION, he says. GIVE ME THE CROWN.

I WON'T, she says.

GIVE IT WILLINGLY, AND I WILL CONSIDER SPARING YOUR BAND OF HUMANS. OF COURSE, WHEN THE LAST REMNANTS OF THIS ISLAND GO UP IN SMOKE, IT IS A LONG DROP TO THE SEA BELOW. I CAN ONLY HOPE THE HALFLING PRINCESS

INHERITED ENOUGH OF HER MOTHER'S DIVINITY TO BREAK THEIR FALL. I SUPPOSE WE'LL FIND OUT VERY SOON.

Panting, teeth bared, Dreamtender stares at him. Her black eyes flick to the ivory statue, then out over the Cloud Sea, where the island fragments are shrinking ever smaller as the eclipse swallows the three moons. She seems to come to a decision.

"No!" Galatea screams. "Don't give it to him!"

Dreamtender lifts her free hand, the one not bound by lightning, to the crown on her head. Skyrender watches with brutal pleasure. THAT'S RIGHT, GODDESS, he says. I KNEW THERE HAD TO BE A MORSEL OF REASON WITHIN YOU SOMEWHERE. NOW, HAND IT OVER.

She looks at him and says:

YOU CANNOT TAKE IT.

Then she rips the crown off her head and hurls it into the air. It sails into the night sky, so small against the stars. Then, at the height of its climb, the Crown of Horn glows bright as a star and bursts into a thousand, thousand pieces. It's like a firework, a cascade of glowing, burning embers that rain down around us and disappear into the clouds, leaving thin trails of smoke behind. One of the pieces hits me right in the chest, a flare of heat that sinks into my skin. I clutch at my heart, gasping, and beside me Sam and Ollie make similar noises of shock and pain. The light fades.

The Crown of Horn has been destroyed.

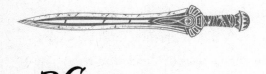

26

A terrible silence fills the aftermath.

Skyrender fixes Dreamtender with a level look. THAT, he says, WAS A MISTAKE.

She spits at him. The gob hits his cheek and slides down into his silver beard.

THAT, TOO. He rises to his feet. Electric sparks crackle at his fingertips. His arm draws back, poised to skewer her with a lightning bolt at point-blank range.

"HEY! BIG GUY!" Ollie shouts at the top of his lungs. A handful of mud flies through the air to smack Skyrender upside the head, splattering all over his face. He goes very still. Slowly, he turns away from Dreamtender and looks

at the four of us. He reaches up to wipe the mud out of his eyes.

HOW ANNOYING.

And he throws the lightning bolt. He's not aiming at Dreamtender. The bolt arcs directly at Ollie, at all of us, searing the air in its path. There's no time to get out of the way. No time to think. Ollie's arms fly up to shield his face—

KRRRRAAACK.

The bolt strikes—but not its target. Something big and white appears out of nowhere to take the hit, exploding into shadows.

"Was that a *sheep*?" says Sam.

Ollie's chest pulses with pale gold light. It's reflecting on the underside of his chin like the glow of a swimming pool. He touches his heart, wide-eyed. Then his gaze travels to Skyrender. "Oh, buddy," he says.

Cloven hooves fill the air.

A wave of sheep bursts forth as if the gates of an invisible paddock have been thrown open. They appear out of nothing, out of shadows, out of darkness itself. Unlike the ones that attacked us outside the Old Barn, these ones don't have feathery black wings. Yet they're still flying, or rather, galloping in thin air. They stream as one toward Skyrender, who, I notice, has finally started to look a bit less bored.

He hurls another lightning bolt. A section of sheep disintegrates with a cloud of sparks, but it barely makes a dent. More sheep flood in to take their place, surrounding Skyrender like a swarm of angry bees until I can't see him through the tornado of wool. They seem to be forcing him backward.

The wind picks up, and a cold rain begins to fall. The moons are half-covered in shadow. We don't have much time. Skyrender's distraction causes the lightning binding Galatea to fizzle out. She pitches forward a little, sucking in huge, shuddering breaths. Her wrists are raw and bubbling with blisters. Then she shakes the hair out of her eyes and draws her sword. It flashes bronze in the storm light.

I grab her shoulder. "Stop! Are you nuts?"

"Let go, Juniper." She turns, face close to mine. I can see rain mixing with sweat on her forehead, grief and fury etched into her features, the freckles on her nose. "I have a score to settle with the king of gods."

"That sword doesn't work for you!"

"I don't care."

She shrugs off my hand and breaks into a run. Skyrender's busy finishing off the last of Ollie's sheep, forks of lightning shooting out of his fingers to disintegrate them ten at a time, and doesn't notice Galatea charging him down until she's already on him. She throws herself at the god, sword bright as the lightning, the stars. There's a spray of golden blood.

Skyrender holds up his arm, examining the fresh stump of his wrist with a sort of vague interest. Molten blood flows from the wound, dripping down to his elbow. Then the stump bulges, and another hand grows to replace the one Galatea severed. Her eyes widen.

YOU MIGHT AS WELL TRY TO CUT DOWN THE SKY, he says.

He shoots a bolt of lightning from his new hand. It strikes the sword and knocks it out of Galatea's grip, sending it flying off the edge of the island. Godkiller hits the clouds and vanishes from sight.

"Galatea!"

She dodges just in time, and a lightning bolt singes her sleeve instead of hitting her square in the chest. Ollie waves an arm. Hundreds of black-winged oneiroi appear in the night sky, swarming above Skyrender's head.

I'M BECOMING TIRED OF YOU MORTALS, he growls, his voice loud as the crashing thunder. Storm clouds are towering in the surrounding sky, flashing with lightning, the atmosphere practically humming with it. The tiny hairs on my arms stand on end. The rain whips at my cheeks. If we can just keep him distracted...Dreamtender's still bound by that blazing rope of lightning, but she's been half crawling, half dragging herself back to the statue of Kypris. Her skin is burning. She's giving off smoke. But there's no pain in her face. There's just furious determination. Cold fire.

"Look out!"

Galatea screams a warning, but it's already too late. A gust of wind sweeps the mountaintop with the force of a hurricane, hitting Sam, Ollie, and me head-on. It's like getting punched by a giant fist. We're thrown backward, away from the ivory statue and off the edge of the island, into the clouds.

We're falling.

I don't scream. I don't even breathe. The storm swallows me instantly. Everything is a blur of gray. I can't see past my own nose. For some incomprehensible reason, the only thing I can think of is how this would look as a comic panel. I imagine myself in free fall with one big, bold exclamation point of shock above my head. The wind batters me back and forth as I plunge through the clouds. Then I drop out of the cloud layer, and suddenly there's the black sheet of the ocean far, far below. Wind whistles in my ears.

A streak of light.

"Aagh!" I land on something huge and firm, grabbing hold on instinct. The impact knocks the breath out of my lungs. Wheezing, I blink the rain out of my eyes.

"You good?" shouts Sam.

I have landed on the back of a giant bird. It's nothing like the bird I rode in a dream that one time—not one of the oneiroi. The bird isn't formed of flesh, bone, and feathers. It's formed of a deep blue-black material that's almost impossible to describe—like silk, smoke, liquid mercury, and like none of those things, solid and gaseous all at once under my hands. It glitters all over, body and wings outlined with flecks of burning white light. Sam's up front, leaning over the bird's neck. Her chest is glowing.

"What is this?" I shout over the storm.

"A constellation!" she says. "The Crane!"

The crane bends its long, graceful neck. I spot the plummeting figure of Ollie in the rain ahead. Sam digs in her heels, and the crane swoops forward, catching him in midair.

"Oof!" he says, and grabs two handfuls of sleek, starlit night, the broad expanse of the crane's back. The crane tilts, climbing higher into the sky. We soar back up through the strobing clouds and into the moonlight...or what's left of it. All three moons are only slivers now. Any moment, the Triple Eclipse will be complete. The third eye will close. The last spark of Kypris's divinity—and any hope of saving the Isle of Kypros and its people—will be lost forever.

The chunk of island holding the statue is now the size of my bedroom, the edges dissolving into smoke. Galatea and Dreamtender have found their way to the statue, clinging on to it so they won't slip and fall off the island. Skyrender's standing balanced on a storm cloud with a lightning bolt in each hand, ready to strike.

"You're a monster!" Galatea's shouting.

MONSTERS ARE MONSTERS, he says. I AM A GOD.

Galatea's jaw drops when she catches sight of us on the

star crane, her look of devastation replaced by pure, wild-eyed hope.

But we're out of time. And Dreamtender can't seem to revive Kypris. She's holding on to the statue, hands on its ivory skin, but nothing's happening. There's no glow, no magic, no flame. No life.

From a distance, over a span of wind and rain, storm clouds and smoke and empty air, I meet Galatea's eyes. My heart throbs. I feel it again—the pull. The tug of a string in my chest, like an unraveling. Time slows. I remember the first time I dreamed of her, the dream that plagued me for weeks: the temple at sunset, golden blood on the mosaics, a sky like an open wound, and the girl beside me, gray eyes, her hand in mine, the calluses on her palm that I now know are from wielding a sword, ivory spreading across her skin. Tooth, bone, shell, a frozen death, her body turned to a cage. I always wanted to tell her, *Wake up. Wake up, be awake, be alive, look at me. I like your eyes, I like the gray of them, how they glint like fish scales in the fading light. Be alive. Be warm and moving, breathing, animate. Wake up. Live.*

I jump off the star crane's back.

I'm flying, hurtling forward. Reaching out desperately,

I manage to catch the statue's hand before the momentum of my fall carries me off the island. The ivory is slippery with rain and moss. I hang on, body twisting in the wind. The ground is rapidly disappearing, going up in multi-colored smoke.

"Juniper!"

Galatea grabs hold of my other hand. Her terrified face fills my vision. An odd light flickers over her, and I realize it's coming from me. My heart is glowing. And so is hers, pulsing once, then twice, then a steady burn. And I know what I have to do.

As the last slivers of moon go dark, I make a wish.

27

For a moment, nothing happens.

There are three black holes in the sky, voids where the moons used to be. The stars shine brightly around them. Skyrender's lightning bolts fizzle out of existence, his powers gone with the eclipse. The storm clears at once, wind and rain dying down.

"No." Dreamtender's clutching the unmoving statue. She buries her face in the white crook of its neck. "No, no, no...."

"What a shame," says Skyrender. "It seems you were unable to save her."

But even as he says it, the cold hand in mine grows warm.

This small patch of earth, barely big enough to hold three people and a statue, is no longer disappearing. There's no more smoke. The crane is hovering nearby, Sam and Ollie on its back, ready to dive and catch us if we fall—but we're not falling. The wet grass under my knees is solid. I scramble to look at Kypris. The ivory is melting away like frost. Tendrils of white fade as quickly as they first appeared, revealing warm skin, soft clothes, the dark fall of her hair. The golden blood is gone. She's whole, unharmed.

Dreamtender lifts her head. "*Oh*," she breathes.

The last flakes of ivory fall away from Kypris's face.

She opens her eyes. Her gaze finds Dreamtender's immediately. Their positions are like a re-creation of the moment before Kypris turned to ivory: Dreamtender's arms wrapped around her, holding her upright, gathering her close. This time, Dreamtender's expression is one of desperate wonder.

Kypris takes a breath. "Hey," she whispers.

"I've had enough of this," Skyrender says. He's now standing on the mountaintop, which is slowly reappearing as Kypris comes back to life. He starts forward with a cold smile. "Four children and two weak, little gods. I don't need divine flame to be rid of you. In fact, this might make it easier."

You know what?

I'm tired of this guy.

I let go of Kypris's and Galatea's hands and get to my feet. "*Juniper!*" Galatea says in a harsh whisper, but I don't answer. I square my shoulders like I've watched her do a million times. I lift my chin defiantly.

The gods lost their powers in the eclipse. But Sam and Ollie are still on that star crane. And I still feel the glow in my chest, like a star nestled beside my heart. A fragment of the Crown of Horn.

I trace a sword-like shape in the air.

It shimmers, and Godkiller appears in my hand. The weapon is fully transformed, its true self, a giant, fiery gold blade. I hold it aloft in the starlight and watch in satisfaction as Skyrender's smug face drains of color.

"What's wrong?" I ask him. "Scared of a mortal?"

He falters. And I realize he was lying when he said he didn't need his divine powers. He was lying to himself. Without his divinity, his thunder and lightning and lashing rain, the godly strength he lords over the people of this world, he's nothing. He's right to be scared of humans. We are so much more than him.

"Every last one of you will regret this," he says.

"Get off my island," Kypris replies.

Skyrender fixes me with a look of burning hatred. "You most of all."

Before I can say anything else, the king of gods is gone. Disappeared into the clouds.

Silence. Then Ollie lets out a yell of triumph, and the star crane swoops down to deposit its riders on the grass. Sam and Ollie come tumbling off it, racing over to me. The crane dissolves into a glimmer of starlight. The three of us turn to Galatea and the two remaining gods, still huddled on the ground. Then Galatea leaps to her feet, hands flying to her mouth.

"Oh!" she gasps. "Oh!"

The Isle of Kypros is reappearing. Land spreads like a green stain over the clouds. The valley swells to meet the hills and mountains, dark peaks rising like a dragon's spine. We can't see past the fully formed mountain range, but I can hear a faint noise in the distance, somewhere beyond. It sounds like bells.

Galatea looks at me. I give her a tiny smile. "Singing cherries," I say.

Silent tears streak down her cheeks.

I go to stand beside her, tilting my head back to gaze up at the trio of moons, the stars burning in their hollows, pinpricks of light set against an infinite, dream-colored dark, a watchful dark. The six of us, young humans and old gods, watch back.

Galatea's home is beautiful.

Silver moonlight breaks over the island like water in shining waves. The eclipse is almost over, shadows slipping off the moons. We're gathered on the mountaintop where the statue of Kypris used to be, where the ruins of her house are now. Godkiller, plain bronze again, is sheathed at Galatea's side.

The two gods stand before us.

YOU MUST RETURN TO YOUR OWN WORLD.

Dreamtender's voice is gentle. She and Kypris are holding hands, fingers intertwined. This close, I can see bits of other colors in Kypris's brown eyes, like flecks of shell and mica in a riverbed. Her face is round and soft, contrasting Dreamtender's sharp angles and long lines. I want to draw them. Together.

"You have my deepest thanks," Kypris says, meeting each of our gazes in turn. "Through your bravery, my island lives, and I as well. Thank you."

THANK YOU, Dreamtender echoes. AND NOW THAT KYPRIS LIVES, SKYRENDER CANNOT STEP FOOT ON THIS ISLAND. IT IS HER DOMAIN AND HERS ALONE.

"I'll tell my people the truth," Galatea says. "I'll tell them everything. About what really caused the drought. About my—my father and his lies. About you, Dreamtender."

The god of dreams almost smiles. YOUR BELIEF IS WORTH MORE THAN YOU KNOW, PRINCESS. AS ARE YOUR DREAMS.

Galatea looks stunned. She nods, seemingly unable to speak.

Then Kypris steps forward. Flowers spring into bloom with each footstep, petals dancing away in the cool, misty breeze. She bends to brush her lips over our foreheads, one at a time. I am completely frozen for it. The only thing I can process is the scent of honey and sunbaked dirt.

I look at Kypris so I don't have to look at Galatea. Even though I want to be looking. I wish I had a sketchbook. We have to go, and she has to stay—but what if I forget the exact shape of her nose, the crooked angle of her rare true grin, the length of her hair? I do want to preserve it. I wouldn't use ivory. Or if I did, I'd paint it well. Because the only way she can exist is in full color, vibrant as a storm at sea.

My gaze catches on Dreamtender's.

DO YOU KNOW WHY IT WAS YOU?

It startles me. Her voice is in my head alone. Time stops, like the god hits some divine pause button. Flower petals hang in the air. Sam's hand is suspended halfway to adjusting her glasses. Only Kypris is unaffected, leaning back from dropping a kiss on Ollie's forehead.

"Why what was me?" I ask.

WHY HER DREAMING MIND FOUND YOURS.

I blink a little. "I—I didn't...wasn't it you? I mean... I haven't had much time to think about it, to be honest. Since learning she was real. I guess I just thought it was a mistake." Even as I say it, I'm thinking about the pull.

I DO NOT BELIEVE IT WAS A MISTAKE.

"Then...what was it? Are you saying we started sharing dreams because we're...connected, somehow?"

I DON'T KNOW is all she says. Then time unfreezes. The flower petals dance away, Sam adjusts her glasses, and the breeze ruffles our hair. The others don't seem to have noticed anything odd. I try not to look shaken. I don't know what I'm supposed to do with this information. What do I do with that? We're leaving. It's time to go home.

"What will you do now?" Galatea asks Dreamtender. "Without the Crown of Horn, how will you return to your island?"

THAT REMAINS TO BE SEEN. FORTUNATELY, HUMANS DON'T NEED ME TO DREAM. YOU MANAGE PERFECTLY WELL ON YOUR OWN.

"The crown was like an extension of the gate, right?" Sam asks. It sounds like she's itching to put her mad scientist brain to work solving this problem.

Galatea nods. "It ferries you back and forth from the Isle of Dreams."

Dreamtender raises an eyebrow. NO, she says.

We all look at her. "What?" says Galatea.

THE CROWN OF HORN COULD OPEN A GATE TO ANYWHERE. YOU SIMPLY HAD TO IMAGINE WHERE

YOU MOST WANTED TO GO AND HOLD THAT DREAM IN YOUR MIND AND HEART.

There's a silence.

Galatea's face is beginning to turn red. It's visible even in the moonlight.

It honestly takes me a couple of moments to catch up. This whole time, we thought she showed up in my bedroom because the Crown of Horn malfunctioned—or, deep down, I thought maybe it was my fault, my embarrassing wish. Could it be that when Galatea put on the Crown of Horn, she thought of me? The girl with the goofy face? Is it possible that, the night she appeared, we thought of each other—wished for each other—at the same time?

Galatea coughs. "...Well!" she says. "Anyway!"

Dreamtender's other eyebrow raises to join the first. She gives me a knowing look. I feel myself blushing, too.

Galatea coughs a second time. Then she faces Sam, Ollie, and me. "Thank you," she says, voice dignified and princess-like again. "For helping me, in your world and in this one. I could never have done it alone. My people, my kingdom, we owe you a great debt."

"Nah," says Ollie, mouth tilting up. "No worries."

"You'd do the same for us," says Sam.

"Yeah," he agrees. "Next time Cypress, South Florida, is in danger of being wiped off the face of the earth, we'll give you a call."

Galatea gives a watery laugh, eyes bright. "And I will come to your aid."

Of course, we don't know if that's true. We don't know what will happen once we return to our own world—if whatever connection that exists between us, and the magic fragments in our hearts, will survive the trip. I can tell we're all thinking it, but no one voices it aloud.

It still feels like a gut punch. A dull, sick thud. I swallow hard.

"We'll miss you," Ollie says. "You're pretty cool, Princess Galatea."

"As are you," she replies, "my friend."

He opens his arms. She steps forward, and he pulls her into a good, strong hug with a thump on the back. Galatea's arms remain stiffly at her sides. I wonder how many times she's been hugged in her royal life. Sam moves in and they embrace, and Galatea manages to pat her hesitantly on the back.

"Bye," Sam says. "Be safe. Be smart."

"You, too," Galatea says, then clears her throat. I realize it's my turn.

"Um." Before I can think better of it, I step in and hook my arms around her shoulders, drawing her into a hug. Her chin clunks against my collarbone. I feel the flutter of her hand on my spine. I squeeze once, then let go. My face burns.

This is it.

COME, MORTALS, says Dreamtender. HOLD ON TO EACH OTHER.

It's time.

We take one another's hands, forming a circle. Just Sam, Ollie, and me. Galatea hangs back, watching. Her jaw is clenched tight. Above us the moons glow, round and full. Around us the island sings.

CLOSE YOUR EYES.

We close our eyes.

FAREWELL, says the god of dreams.

The color behind my eyelids goes pitch-black.

28

One month later

H ow do I look?"

Ollie strikes a pose in the bathroom doorway. His costume mostly resembles a pile of gooey green snot. He's just finished painting his face green to match.

"So good," I say.

He bats a hand at me. "Aw, shucks."

We return to my bedroom to find Sam smoothing the front of her Ghostbuster jumpsuit and adjusting the straps of her proton pack. Ollie is, of course, the ghost.

I'm dressed as a black cat, which basically just means I'm wearing all black and a cat-ear headband, plus I drew whiskers on my cheeks.

Tonight is the Halloween dance. As you can imagine, Mom was thrilled when I asked if my friends could get ready at our house. She made a batch of pumpkin-chocolate-chip cookies, and I supervised in the kitchen to make sure she didn't go rogue with the spices. Next to the crumb-covered plate on my desk, there's a stack of sketches for my webcomic *Cicadaland*. I've been working on it constantly this past month, around school and homework and hanging out with Sam, Ollie, and their other friends. I'm almost done with part one, which tells the story of how the cicada and honeybee meet.

I haven't dreamed for a month. Well—that's not true. I've definitely had some anxiety dreams about failing tests and embarrassing myself at school. But it's just normal stuff. If Galatea and I are connected, it hasn't shown. The only thing that's changed since returning from the Isle of Kypros—besides, you know, everything—is that Sam, Ollie, and I have retained tiny bits of our magic. It's a lot less powerful here. It's taken us weeks of practice to make the fragments in our chests glow, and we still can't do much with them. But who knows? Maybe someday we'll be able to summon nightmares and constellations, portals and dreams.

I take it back. I did sort of have one dream about Galatea. It involved her voice coming out of a fluffy gray cat, and all she said was: "Are you serious, Juniper?" And then I woke up. Something tells me that dream wasn't cosmically significant.

Mom appears at the door. "Oh, don't y'all look fabulous!" she says, beaming at the three of us in our costumes. "Ready for photos? Ollie, your mama made me promise I'd take a bunch. And if we leave in ten minutes, you'll be fashionably late."

So, we take a bunch of photos. So, we pile into the car, and Mom drives us through the streets of Cypress, jack-o'-lanterns winking from front porches, crows shuffling on the telephone wires. So, we pull into the parking lot of Franklin B. Pruitt and join the crowd of costumed kids trickling into the gym. It looks the same as it did last time, except now the streamers dangling from the basketball hoops are black and orange and there are fake cobwebs taped to the walls. The disco ball glitters overhead. DJ Coach J is set up with his laptop and speakers, playing an EDM remix of the *Ghostbusters* theme song, so Sam and Ollie immediately rush the dance floor.

I follow them.

We dance for a while, hopping up and down and cackling with laughter when Sam shows off her skills at doing the robot. We take breaks to eat cookies and fun-sized candy bars and drink orange punch. Caramel sticks in my back teeth. Noah and Kamaria find us on the dance floor, Noah dressed as a goth cowboy, Kamaria in a green cloak with rubber elf ears. Then "Party Rock Anthem" fades out into the first strains of a slow song. Everyone around us starts pairing off.

"I'm gonna get some punch," I tell no one in particular.

I make a beeline for the snack table. But I don't actually want punch. I want to be somewhere quiet. So, like last time, I slip past the parent chaperones and escape the gym, heading down the hall and out a side door into the balmy night. I don't need to go cry in the art room. I just need a minute to breathe.

It's October, but autumn in Florida is not a thing. The

air is hot and soupy, and moths and mosquitoes are buzzing around the yellow sodium lights. I take a deep breath. In four, out four.

"Juniper."

I go very still. That voice.

Then, slowly, I turn around.

I gape at her. "Am I... is this a dream?"

Galatea, standing there on the sidewalk, rolls her eyes. "Obviously not. After all we've been through, you still can't tell the difference between a dream and reality? Thundering skies, Juniper. Of course this isn't a dream. I'm not a cat this time, am I?" Her eyes flick over me, taking in the whiskers and headband. "However, it seems we've switched roles. Is there a reason you're wearing cat ears?"

I scrape together enough brain cells to respond. "Wait. You... when I had that dream—the fluffy cat—that was actually you?"

"I was *trying* to communicate with you. It didn't work. Partially my fault—I haven't mastered the dreaming magic yet. I've been catching glimpses of your dreams all month. Lots of bees. The ones from your drawings, yes?"

"You recognized my bees?"

"Of course I recognized your bees. Shut up," she says

reflexively. "A fluffy cat, though? Really? Your mind is a wonder. And you still haven't explained the ears."

"Today's Halloween," I say faintly. "It's, um, a holiday. Where you dress up in a costume. I'm, um. I'm a cat."

"I gathered that much. Your whiskers are smeared, by the way."

I just shake my head. "How are you here?"

Maybe I'm imagining it, but I think her eyes soften. "I told you, I haven't mastered the dreaming magic yet. It took me a while to figure this part out, but I did."

"What part?"

"How to walk the pathways between worlds. How to—how to imagine where I most want to go and hold that dream in my mind and heart."

It hangs in the air. *Where I most want to go.* My throat is dry. I should've had some punch after all. "Then—then—you're here. You can come here."

"It seems that way," she says. "And, Juniper...we didn't have a chance to talk after the battle, but I wanted to apologize."

"Oh, no, you don't—"

"*Juniper. Please.*"

I shut my mouth.

"Thank you," she says. "I told you once I would never treat you callously, and then I proceeded to do exactly that. I was cruel to you, again. That morning, I said a great many things I regret. I said them out of fear. You were right: I was afraid to admit I was wrong. I called you a coward, but the truth is that you were never the frightened one. I was. I was the coward, and—and after everything I said, you still risked your life to come after me in the Isle of Dreams, to save me when I was determined to do something foolish and reckless, and...I suppose I just want to say...I'm sorry." She takes a steadying breath. "Juniper of Cypress, you are perhaps the bravest person I have ever met. I owe you my life. I'm sorry. Thank you."

I can feel my ears burning. "Um," I manage. "I—I forgive you. And, um, I'm sorry, too."

She frowns. "What do you have to apologize for?"

"I don't know!" I squeak. "Something! I don't know!"

"You're very strange." Then her gaze drifts behind me. "What is that noise?"

"Huh?" I listen. I can hear the thumping music from the gym. "O-oh. Yeah. So, there's kind of a dance going on."

"A dance?" She looks interested. "Are the others here?"

"Yeah, they're inside," I say. My heart's still fluttering from her apology speech. *The bravest person I have ever met*, she said. "Wanna go in?"

"Do I need a costume?"

I look at her. Galatea is wearing a deep purple chiton under a twilight-blue robe made of a flowy material that looks lighter than silk, plus leather sandals and a gold circlet on her forehead. There's a sword sheathed at her waist, but I don't think it's Godkiller—the hilt is wrapped leather, not bronze. I have a feeling Godkiller is hidden away somewhere safe.

"Actually, I think you're good," I tell her. "Also, please do not take out the sword when we're in there. If anyone asks, it's made of plastic."

Together, we head back inside to the gym. The slow song is over. Bass is vibrating up through the soles of my sneakers, and colorful lights are flashing. Galatea takes it in with huge eyes. There's so much I want to ask her, so much I want to talk about—but for now, I think I just want to dance. We find Sam and Ollie at the snack table. Sam nearly drops a cup of punch when she sees Galatea.

"WHAT!" she shouts, and Ollie spins around, lets

out a whoop, and wraps Galatea in a joyful bear hug that leaves a smudge of green paint on her cheek.

"WHAT!" Sam shouts again, laughing. "WHAT!"

The four of us hit the dance floor. The crowd bounces like popcorn. When the song changes, Galatea leans into my ear. "What legend is this song referring to?" she asks over the music. "It sounds like an epic tale of the greatest heroes of your realm!"

The song playing is "Monster Mash."

The zombies were having fun,
the party had just begun
The guests included Wolfman,
Dracula, and his son....

"Yeah," I reply. "Yeah, it is."

At one point, a few of us go to the bathroom. We keep laughing for no reason. If there's a joke, I don't remember it. Or maybe the joke is how strange it is to walk through the dark halls after hours, or the parent chaperones doing their dorky disco moves—my dad would totally approve—or one of Kamaria's elf ears falling off into the toilet. Maybe the joke is all of us crowding into the bathroom and checking our painted faces in the mirror, streaked and shiny with sweat. The joke is Sam swatting us with the nozzle of her proton pack and Galatea's fascination with the automated paper towel dispenser and Ollie's increasingly desperate attempts to get DJ Coach J to play a headbanger. It's all of that and none of it. What matters is, I'm laughing so hard my ribs hurt.

We return to the gym, to the music and lights. Before I know it, DJ Coach J is saying into a microphone, "Okay, folks. It's nine fifty PM, which means my bedtime was an hour ago. This is the second to last song."

Strums of acoustic guitar fill the gym. Everyone scrambles to find partners and shuffle into position. Sam twirls Ollie before drawing him into a dramatic waltz. Within moments, almost the whole crowd is paired off, and suddenly there's a lot of empty space on either side of me and Galatea. My heart's pounding. She's avoiding my eyes.

God. Oh my god. Okay.

"Do you wanna dance with me?" I blurt out. My voice cracks on the word *dance*. My cheeks are aflame. If she says no, I might just run out of the gym into the night, never to be seen again.

"All right," she says.

"Oh." I wheeze out a breath. "Oh. Cool. Okay, yeah. Let's, um..."

We face each other. Mirroring the other pairs, Galatea's hands come up to settle on my waist. I rest my hands on her shoulders, praying they're not so sweaty she'll be able to feel it through her clothes. Then...we're swaying back and forth. We're slow dancing. I can feel the heat of her palms through my shirt. I think of how honeybees, upon finding a new patch of wildflowers, return to the hive and do these butt-wiggling dances to tell the other bees where to go. They draw maps with their little honeybee feet. This way, go this way, you'll find flowers.

We turn slowly to the croon of some country singer, tracing half-moon patterns on the gym floor. I catch the scent of her hair over the mingled smells of sweat and deodorant and boy cologne, sweet like honeysuckle, dark and salty like the sea. I can't bring myself to meet her eyes. Instead, I'm staring hard at her left ear, her collarbone, a random spot past her shoulder. Her hands are so warm. I'm so aware of those two points of contact, the way my sides rise and fall with my breaths. Is this what it felt like for Riley when she danced with those boys? How did she bear it? I feel neon. I'm too nervous to check if Galatea's trying to look at me, if she's looked at me even once. I can't tell if she feels as electric as I do. I'm scared to find out either way.

I kind of want the song to end, but only because I'm about to implode.

I've missed you, I don't say. *Galatea, I've really missed you.*

But I don't want to risk severing it, this burning thread between us, so I keep my mouth shut. It feels like both a thousand years and only a brief moment before DJ Coach J is booming, "Aaaaand last one! Happy Halloween!"

The acoustic guitar changes to a bouncy pop song. Galatea and I let go of each other, hands falling away. Then Sam and Ollie are on us again, and the others follow, surrounding us with a pulsing circle of friends. Everyone's teeth are glowing with their wild grins. I can't help it—I laugh, too. And so does Galatea, tossing her head back, the brightest I've ever seen her. Sweaty and exhilarated, knocking elbows, we dance to the last song of the night.

Just before the overhead lights come on, I close my eyes. I think of how I'd draw this moment, how I'd capture it:

hot color and swirling light, the crowd's hands waving like sea creatures in a current, the floor tilted at a dizzy angle. The shapes of our bodies, whole and lopsided and sliding together like puzzle pieces. For the first time in my life, I feel like a perfect fit.

EPILOGUE

Galatea of Kypros can't sleep.

For hours she's been lying awake, watching the light of three moons slide across the floor of her bedchamber. Beyond the tower walls, the Cloud Sea roars and the wind howls like it always does this high in the sky. These are the sounds she's fallen asleep to her whole life, the sounds she finds most calming in all the world (all the *worlds*), yet tonight they're grating on her nerves. She scowls up at the ceiling. There's no reason to have trouble sleeping these days. It's not like she's still having the dreams.

And, she reminds herself sternly, she certainly doesn't

miss the dreams. They were confusing. And frightening. It's not like she needs to see Juniper's bug-eyed expression each night in order to lift her spirits and remind her to stop and breathe sometimes, or anything ridiculous like that. Of course not.

(It's been three days since she returned from visiting the other world, and she's only just been able to stop thinking about that dance. The slow dance. Juniper's light hands and pink face. It's terrible. Galatea has *duties*.)

She rolls over for the hundredth time, despairing. It will be dawn soon, and with dawn will come another long day of speaking to people older and wiser than their child princess, people who clearly think her unfit for the throne, who flatter and cajole her while barely suppressing the distrust in their eyes....

Was that a shadow outside the window?

Galatea sits bolt upright, hand creeping in the direction of her sword, which she keeps right beside the bed. She watches the window; the light, fluttering curtains. The night sky is peaceful, starry. She waits for a ten count. Then another. All is still. Slowly, she lowers herself back onto the pillows.

Something collides with the side of the tower hard

enough to rattle her entire bedchamber. Scrolls and papers go rolling off the desk. Galatea leaps out of bed and grabs her sword. Hand on the hilt, prepared to draw, she approaches the large, moonlit window. Her bedchamber is at the very top of the north tower. Whatever's out there must be airborne. Could it be the oneiroi? Perhaps the god of dreams found reason to send a message?

A face appears outside the window. Galatea freezes. The breath stops in her lungs. She forgets the sword, the room around her, *everything*, and stares.

"I hope I didn't wake you."

The woman's voice is unknown and familiar all at once.

As if in a trance, Galatea goes to the window and looks out into the night. The woman is sitting on the back of a sea dragon. Its long, shimmering body twists like a green river suspended hundreds of feet in the air, its powerful wings—like fins—beating hard to keep it aloft. Its visible eye burns gold.

"Galatea," says her mother. "Your father's in danger. Get on."

Author's Note

This book is inspired by the story of Pygmalion and the Statue, best known from Ovid's *Metamorphoses* (first published circa 8 CE). Ovid, a Roman writer, dramatized and popularized a story he'd read in the now-lost text *De Cypro*, a history of the island of Cyprus published two hundred years earlier. *De Cypro* was written by Philostephanus of Cyrene, a writer in ancient Greece.

In Book X of *Metamorphoses*, the bard Orpheus sings the tale of Pygmalion and the Statue, which goes something like this:

Once there was an artist named Pygmalion who lived on the island of Cyprus. Pygmalion had desperate want of a wife, but he hated all the women in his town, whom he viewed as wicked and not fit to be married. To ease his loneliness, Pygmalion carved a statue of a woman out of ivory...then fell in love with his own creation. He courted the statue, bringing her gifts and flowers and dressing her up in fine clothes, and even kissed her. Then, one day, the island of Cyprus held a festival for Aphrodite, the goddess of love. Pygmalion knelt at Aphrodite's altar and made a wish: "I wish for a bride like my ivory woman." Aphrodite heard his wish and, taking pity on him, decided to grant it. When Pygmalion returned home, he kissed his statue as usual—and her lips grew warm under his own. His kiss brought her to life, transforming her from a statue into a real, living woman. The ivory woman blushed pink as she gazed back at Pygmalion. They were wed, with Aphrodite in attendance, and lived happily ever after.

(Quick aside: Pygmalion's statue remained nameless until Jean-Jacques Rousseau, a philosopher in the eighteenth century, wrote the theatrical work *Pygmalion*. In his play, Rousseau named the statue Galatea—he took the name from an unrelated Greek mythological figure, Galatea the sea nymph, who features in the myth of Acis and Galatea. Since then, the statue has been referred to as Galatea and the story as "the myth of Pygmalion and Galatea.")

In the two thousand years since *Metamorphoses*, the tale of Pygmalion and the Statue has been told and retold, reinterpreted and reimagined, countless times. It has inspired plays and poems and paintings, sculptures and songs, novels, films, and so on. Like many before me, I read the original story (well, Ovid's version of it) and wondered: What was it like for the statue?

That was the seed of this book—that question and those that came after: How does it feel for an object to become animate, for a statue to be granted spirit and flesh? How about the lonely creator who inadvertently wishes someone into existence? (What if that *someone* already existed?) I thought about fantasy crashing into reality, with all its flaws. Then I covered those thoughts with monsters and middle school and the agony of a first crush, and here we are. Thank you for reading.

ACKNOWLEDGMENTS

This is the shortest book I've ever written, and also for some reason the hardest to write. (I think probably the "some reason" had a lot to do with there being a pandemic on. Yeah.) To the following people, please know that when I thank you, I am not only thanking you for whatever role you played in helping me write this book; I am thanking you deeply and from the bottom of my screaming cicada heart for being my beloved friend and/or family member; I am thanking god(s) and the cosmos that you're in my life. These past few years have been progressively more and more frightening, devastating, exhausting, et cetera, for each and every one of us on varying levels. Thank you for being here anyway, despite.

All this to say, thank you to Kieryn for the hours of plot talk and everything else talk, for being my forever 'n' ever pal, my twin flame. Thank you to Piera for being astonishingly good and wise; to Tony for being way hip and cool(er than me); to Papa and Mama for never once giving me reason to doubt your love and acceptance; to Fiona and Paul for your belief. To Ivy, thank you for your unwavering ability to sense my vibes; for sharing with me your mind, your writing, your fierce love. To Amy, thank you for being my #1 hype man; I am hyping you in return; thank you for the coffee shop seshes and rom-com nights. To the IRLs (I can't put the chat name here but YKWYA): thank you for being the warmest, wackest, funniest people on the planet, for doing and making all the myriad cool things you do. To LP (pretend I tried to order you by birth year but got it totally wrong): thank you for teaching me more about storytelling, craft, and friendship with every passing year. To all other friends and family, thank you, I love you.

Now the professional stuff. To my brilliant agent Patrice Caldwell: thank you for your passion and genius brain, your knowledge and advice (which is literally always right), for being my first and fiercest advocate. Triple thank you to my editor Alexandra Hightower: I put you through the wringer with this one, as I figured out what I wanted this story to do and be, and it absolutely wouldn't exist if not for you and your incredibly thoughtful editorial work through the entire process. You saw the vision from the start and in every iteration since; I can't thank you enough for helping craft this story at every stage, for always believing in it. You're the best. Thank you to the team at Little, Brown Books for Young Readers: Bill Grace, Andie Divelbiss, Shivani Annirood, Christie Michel, Amber Mercado, Annie McDonnell, and Virginia Lawther; thank you to Veronica Grijalva, Victoria Henderson, and the rest of the New Leaf Literary & Media team; thank you to rock star Trinica Sampson for your hard work in regards to this book and (wink) other projects. For the cover, thank you to Jenny Kimura for the type and design; thank you to Maike Plenzke for your gorgeous art upon which I have been gazing in adoration for months now. I am so lucky to work with all of you.

Finally, last but certainly not least: thank you, the reader, especially the kids, especially-especially the queer kids (the ones who know and the ones who don't yet; every one of you). I am grown-up and queer and alive&happy and I love you. I wrote this book for you. I want to tell you: The past can feel as distant as another world, as colorless as a marble statue with all the paint worn off. But it wasn't. It was vibrant, chaotic, fluid, alive. People have always been just as human as they are now. Cultural context (as in, what is considered "normal" versus what is considered, say, "queer") may differ vastly, but people have always loved how we love. "Queer" people have always existed—and thus have always found and loved each other, carved out sacred spaces for ourselves. Queerness is a tapestry that stretches backward and forward into infinity, woven from millions of threads. Your life adds to that splendor. Everything you feel and do and make matters. It matters that you're here. I'm so glad you are. The world can be scary and cruel, but I promise: Love awaits you. There will be (if there aren't already) people who know you past your bones to the red of your heart and love you for every bit of it, everything you are. Such happiness exists; it is real; you can find it. For now, thank you for being in this world. Let's stay here together for a long time. Let's shape ourselves and each other and the world around us with careful hands. It's all for you: your stubborn flame, your heart-fire, burning ever brighter as you grow, transform, and become your truest self. Tend it well for me, okay? For you. Thank you.